DARK

Submissions

LAUREL CREMANT

WINGED MOON
PUBLISHING

Dark Submissions
Copyright © 2016 by Laurel Cremant

ISBN: 978-0-9916357-6-4

Cover Art by Taria Reed Digital Artist
Print First Edition

Winged Moon Publishing, LLC
Hollywood, Florida

This is a work of fiction. Names, characters, places, and incidents either are the product of the author's imagination or are used fictitiously, and any resemblance to actual persons living or dead, business establishments, events or locales, is entirely confidential.

Love doesn't exist only in the light. Travel to the Underworld and get lost in the dark with two erotic tales of sensuality, lust, and the quest to find love...

DEATH'S HOPE

The dating scene in Hell is rough for a woman who embodies the essence of pure hope, but Dora is trusting that death demon, Alphonse, won't mind introducing her to a little sin. Her plan to convince Alphonse she's no innocent demon-in-training, takes a wicked turn, when Alphonse decides to show her exactly how decadent his needs are.

GUILT'S PLEASURE

Vengeance demon, Morgan, is looking for a little relief from a guilty conscious, and fire demon, Dax, has just the remedy for her within the walls of his dungeon. A simple bargain for relief turns sensual, when Dax realizes Morgan needs more from him than a steady hand and a long whip.

For all of you who understand love can be found even in the darkest of places...

Death's

HOPE

One

*H*overing outside the great doors of Bacchus's pleasure palace, Dora took a deep measuring breath.

Time to explore my wicked side.

She smiled at the encouraging thought bouncing through her mind, but her muscles remained frozen with hesitation. Clenching and unclenching her fists at her sides, she reviewed her plan yet again.

This has to work.

She'd spent weeks contemplating her options, but when she'd learned that Bacchus, a chief vice demon, was hosting another one of his feasts, she knew it would be the perfect opportunity. Replaying her plan again in her mind, she winced at some of the points, then firmed her chin against any doubts. True, it wasn't foolproof. The plot was filled with several unknowns, but she still hoped for a satisfactory outcome.

A part of her worried about the repercussions of her plan,

but she shoved those thoughts aside. Once she'd made up her mind, both nervousness and anticipation settled in her bones.

Taunting death wasn't something anyone should do lightly.

Her nipples pebbled at that thought. That was the source of all her problems. All she wanted was to taunt Alphonse, the high demon known as Death. To tease the stubborn demon into fucking her senseless.

Towering tall and thickly built, Alphonse had a physique that made her mouth water. In mockery to his role of death dealing, the Gods blessed him with thick blond hair and golden hued skin that stretched taut over large hardened muscles.

His handsome face consisted of full lips beneath a strong slash of a nose which Alphonse took pleasure looking down at others from with his mercury colored eyes. A long scar dipped from the corner of his left eye down to the top of the same cheek.

Dora shook her head. As if his face and body weren't beautiful enough, Alphonse's root form consisted of a long, golden scaled tail. It was over five feet in length. In battle he wielded the thick extension like an additional weapon.

In bed, he reportedly did the same.

Shivering, she recalled the stories she'd heard of the wicked things Alphonse did to his lovers with his extra appendage. Frowning, she thought of all the times they'd been alone together. His tail remained hidden behind his back without a single twitch of interest.

Fighting down the urge to grind her teeth, she blew out a quick breath.

For months she'd endured his placid treatment. He claimed to care for her, but hid his passion from her as if she were a chaste nun.

"I'm no shrinking virgin," she said, her lips pulling down in a frown.

She enjoyed sex, craved it even. Physical touch and signs of affection were tools of empathy—an emotion that fed her powers and kept her strong. Most demons in the Underworld didn't understand how powerful the act of touch was. The intimacy of a single caress, offered in affection or love, was a powerful thing. She didn't need it to survive, not like the succubus demons, but it did boost her strength.

She'd never experienced a touch like Alphonse's.

The first time his skin brushed against hers she'd held her breath, wanting the delicious moment to last forever. His rough fingers had grazed across hers and cradled her hand in his palm. The slow slide of friction, causing goosebumps to radiate from that point of contact and center at her pussy. Wet heat coated her labia as he gave a slight bow and brought her hand up to his lips for a kiss.

"*We meet at last.*"

Even now, she didn't know how she replied to his husky

introduction. It had taken every ounce of will not to strip naked and throw herself at his feet. Since then, she'd seen him almost every day.

She'd learned what made him laugh, what intrigued his keen intellect. He was several millennia old, and his mind still sought out enigmas and puzzles. She loved the deep-raspy sound of his voice, the firm slant of his jaw, and the way his cheek twitched when he was angry.

She craved his touch, his smiles and kind gestures, but most of all she craved *all* of him—including the pieces he attempted to hide.

As a death demon, Alphonse had a dark side he tried to mask from her. In the beginning, she'd been too enamored by the him to notice his hesitancy. However, as the days and weeks wore on, she'd fallen in love with him and wanted to know every facet of him. Looking at back on that time now, she was sure her mind took that time to catch up to what her heart knew that first instant he took her hand.

She hoped he loved her as well, but knowing he held a piece of himself back prevented her from reveling her full feelings to him. They still hadn't even made love. Every time things became heated, he pulled away, kissed her gently, then left her and himself unfulfilled.

She hadn't even had the opportunity to see his cock.

He kept that just as well under guard as his feelings, but what she'd felt of him pressed up against her, filled her dreams. There, she was allowed to tease and pleasure her demon to completion.

For a while, her dreams and manual stimulation kept her frustration at bay, but Dora yearned for the real thing. From the beginning, she dreamed of him touching her, spreading her legs wide and tasting her there. Every morning she woke up with her hands between her thighs covered in her own arousal.

It ends today.

She was tired of waiting for Alphonse to stop treating her like some delicate flower. If she was ever going to convince him that she wanted more than tepid kisses and gentle loving, it would be tonight.

Her body tingled at that thought. Tonight, Alphonse's best friend, Bacchus, was hosting yet another feast at his palace, and Dora had arranged to attend. The feasts were known to be decadent, wild occasions, full of drink and erotic sexual encounters. Dora had never been interested in attending, but she knew her presence there would alert Alphonse. If Bacchus didn't inform him, then his loyal foot soldiers would.

Even now she felt their presence hovering behind her.

Specters.

Soldiers who were valiant fighters in life and had sworn their allegiance to Alphonse in death. From the day he first began courting her she'd known the wraith-like guards followed and observed her movements within the

Underworld. No doubt, it was Alphonse's way of protecting her. He shouldn't have bothered.

Like Alphonse, she was a *pithos* demon. A demon that embodied one of the many troubles and sins let loose by Pandora and her infernal jar. As the embodiment of hope, Dora was rarely unwelcome in the dark realm of the Underworld. She felt more at home traveling through Hell than anywhere else. No one ever seemed to understand that her powers thrived in darkness.

A slight shift in the air behind her alerted Dora that her shadow guards were getting restless. No doubt they were unsure of why she'd traveled here.

She hovered outside the doors of Bacchus' palace a moment longer, her lips curling upwards before taking a deep breath and releasing it in a huff. Reaching up, she pushed back her hood and unclasped the tie at her neck. The heavy garment fell to the floor leaving her naked.

With a smile she looked over her shoulders and smiled in the direction she knew the guards stood.

"Go find your master and tell him I'm tired of waiting."

Facing the doors again, she pushed them open and stepped into the great hall of sin.

two

Alphonse had visited every level of Hell during his lifetime in the Underworld as the bringer of death. Very few beings or things surprised him, and even fewer elicited an emotional response from him—until today. Gyrating in front of a crowded hall of revelers and spectators, was Dora—his innocent little hope of a demon.

When his guards informed him of her presence here, he didn't want to believe them. He'd assumed it was their attempt at a terrible joke—but the worried looks on their faces had propelled him to action.

Over the last several months, his bodyguards had grown attached to Dora. That didn't surprise Alphonse. Dora had such a pure heart, it was difficult for anyone to dislike her. Her genuine want to bring light to the darkest parts of Vinghel's realm, Hell, was hard to ignore.

It was her innocence that first drew him to her—that made him take a longer look at the small demon. Like the quality she embodied, Dora at first appeared unassuming, but the more he observed her, the more remarkable she became.

Her small stature, often cloaked by heavy robes, hid luscious curves that played hide and seek each time she moved. He would watch her cross the main courtyards, captivated by how the gentle sway of her hips betrayed the hint of her high rounded ass.

At first glance, her hair appeared to be a deep-red, but on closer inspection, her wild mop of curls contained at least a hundred different shades of red and brown, each one catching the light in different ways. The first time he'd met her in person, his palms had itched to grasp the back of her head and slip his fingers around the silky strands.

Her dark skin shone like chocolate dipped in amber, as if the Gods understood that such perfection should be preserved and admired. Alphonse couldn't count the times he'd spent wondering about its softness or how it would feel pressed against him.

Her mouth...

Alphonse clenched his teeth at the images streaking through his brain. Every time he focused on her lips, he imagined them wrapped around his cock sucking him dry or open wide on a scream as he fucked her until she couldn't breathe.

Of all her features, her eyes were his downfall. The

moment those warm-amber orbs peered up at him with a heady combination of trust and lust, Alphonse knew he was lost—and that was his dilemma.

For all her innocence and purity, all Alphonse wanted to do was make her dirty. He wanted her in every decadent way imaginable, every hole filled, every position taken.

The first time he'd approached her and she offered a tentative hello, he'd been lost. He courted her from that moment on, determined to bind her to him, even when he knew his dark soul didn't deserve hers.

When they held hands and went on long walks, he wanted to push her down on all fours and rut her for hours. When he kissed her softly at night he wanted to pull her closer and devour her mouth before burying his head between her legs and feasting on her pussy.

He marveled at the fact that others didn't see how sexy she was. Every time he saw or thought of her, he grew hard with arousal. Where others saw a symbol of hope, he saw a woman so innocently sexy, she was made for sin.

Alphonse didn't know if he could control himself with her. Fear of hurting her plagued him. He liked his sex kinky and rough. Centuries of seeing the worst of humanity had taught him to take his pleasure with zeal. He didn't know if Dora was up for his particular brand of loving. So he'd been taking it slow, waiting for a sign that she would be interested in something more than gentle loving.

Perhaps now I have my answer.

Now that woman, danced among a crowd of drunks, exposing the body he coveted to a hall full of intoxicated fools.

They'll die.

Alphonse stood at the end of the ballroom and watched the crowd with a hooded gaze. They sat and stood in various forms of undress throughout the great hall as they engaged in all levels of debauchery. The room smelled of smoke, wine and sex. The scents mingled together to produce a wanton fragrance that was at once intoxicating and sinful.

In the past, Alphonse enjoyed attending these types of parties, but since Dora, he could only imagine indulging with her.

As a testament to the party-goers' level of inebriation, no one seemed to notice his presence. Which was a good thing, since he wanted to kill each and every one of them, and at the top of his list was Bacchus, his soon to be very dead friend.

He seethed as they watched her. *His* woman.

Balling his fists at his sides, he attempted to rein in his temper, but knew his silver eyes were already hazed over to black. His nails elongated and curved into sharp talons and the air around him began to chill and frost.

Those closest to him shifted away, the small sober portions of their brains attempting to move them to safety.

Dora undulated on the dais, her hands roaming up her body and cupping her magnificent breasts. They were as gorgeous as he'd imagined. Her skin gleamed with a hint of sweat, the thin rivulets skimming down her chest, abdomen and thighs, while her pussy was bare and smooth, glistening in the low light.

Everyone's gaze was on her as she danced. Her hips swayed and rocked back and forth as if she was riding a hard cock between her legs.

His own dick hardened even as his anger grew. He imagined her over him riding him until he exploded into her. Knowing the others imagined the same, he growled low.

Propelling to action, he approached her, bringing the cold with him, the crowd grew silent.

"*Ahhh.* We have another unexpected visitor. Alphonse my friend, welcome to the celebration!"

Bacchus stood from his mass of pillows lain across the floor and clapped his hands together as if nothing was amiss. Alphonse spared the demon lord a withering glare before returning his attention to Dora.

She stilled, her hips frozen in a provocative slant. Then, in a slow twist, she straightened and turned to him in a careful pirouette.

Her long hair floated around her shoulders like a cloak. The dark mass serving as the perfect frame to her beautiful face.

"Hello Alphonse," she said.

He scowled at her blank expression for a moment before speaking.

"What are you doing here?"

He enunciated the words in slow precision. With his blood pounding a rapid rhythm at his temples, he needed to make sure she heard him correctly.

She shrugged, the action making the ample globes of her breasts sway and jiggle.

"I've never been to one of Bacchus's parties and decided to pop in."

He felt a tick tug at his scarred cheek.

"Pop in?"

"*Hmm.*"

She flicked at her hair, stepped from the dais, and walked towards him. Each step she took brought the swaying perfection of her body into hyper clarity. The room around him began to blur, bringing Dora into hyper-focus.

"They are all watching you, lusting after what's mine," he said between clenched teeth.

"Yours?"

She raised a delicate brow at him, her pouty lips pursing down into a frown.

"First. I'm no one's pet or a thing you can possess. Second, even if I felt like allowing a limited lease...I don't recall you staking a claim. As a matter of fact, I'm sure I would distinctly remember it if you did."

He hissed out a breath and tried to hold back a snarl.

What was wrong with her? She knew his feelings--knew he cared about her. Why would she pretend otherwise?

He flicked his gaze towards Bacchus who was observing them with wide eyes.

"What have you given her?" he asked Bacchus.

As a vice demon, Bacchus often laced his food and wine with spells and enchantments geared towards lowering inhibitions. It was the only plausible explanation for Dora's behavior.

Bacchus raised his hands up to his shoulders, palms facing outward.

"Not a single thing. I welcomed her to the hall, but made sure nothing she drank would affect her. I know you...hold her in affection."

The demon had the nerve to curl his lips in a smile. The bastard knew Alphonse held Dora in more than just a light fondness. He was enjoying seeing Alphonse lose his temper. Unfurling his fingers from his palms, Alphonse held back the impulse to pummel Bacchus to the ground.

"Then how would you explain this?"

Alphonse waved his hand at Dora, his cool a distant memory. Bacchus replied with a shrug of his own.

"You know I *am* standing right here. You could just ask me yourself."

Alphonse returned his attention to Dora, glaring at her continued mocking tone. The air around him chilled a few more degrees. If she continued testing his patience, he feared his control would slip entirely.

Just as quickly as the thought occurred to him, he watched a shiver work its way up her body. It prickled her smooth skin in a tantalizing sweep and pebbled her nipples. He licked his lips, distracted by the notion of what the sensitive breasts would taste like in his mouth.

"Your nipples are hard."

He winced at his blunt words. What the hell was wrong with him? He was letting her body distract him when he should be wrapping his cloak around her body and dragging her away from Bacchus and his depraved party. Reaching for the gold clasp at his throat he began to do just that.

"I know," she said, jutting her chin out at him. "They tend to get that way around you."

The cloak almost slipped from his fingers at her response. He clenched his jaw at the sound of Bacchus chuckling behind him.

"You shouldn't say things like that," he told her.

"And why is that?" she asked.

Placing a hand on her hip, she tilted her head and stared at him, her dark eyes blinking up at him in an innocent flutter. He wasn't fooled. Narrowing his eyes, he firmed his grip on the material in his hands, and with a flick of his wrists, draped the heavy garment around her shoulders.

"Because you don't realize that you're asking for something you're not ready for," he said.

"What if I do?"

"You don't."

Securing the clasp around her neck and gathering the sides of the material around her shoulders, Alphonse felt some measure of calm return as her curves disappeared from view.

Her hands closed on top of his, stilling his movements.

" *They* all see me as a desirable woman," she said.

Her dark eyes flashed a bright red before slipping back to their natural brown in gradual shades. Before he could react to her anger, a quick look of sadness crossed her face. Before he could examine it further, she schooled her features and pushed his hands away.

"Dora—"

He said her name in warning, his jaw clenching as she stepped away from him. She unclasped the cloak and let it fall to the floor.

"Maybe one of them is willing to touch me instead of acting like I'll break—"

" *Enough.* "

His yell echoed through the hall, the force of it making the crowd blink at them, signs of sobriety finally lighting their eyes.

Self-preservation would do that.

They all understood what would happen if he lost his

temper, the harm he could cause—all except the foolish woman in front of him. She didn't even pause in her retreat.

"Alphonse, you're ruining the party."

Alphonse didn't turn his head at Bacchus's complaint.

"Be lucky I consider you a friend and don't tear you apart where you stand," he said to Bacchus.

His friend snorted.

"You used to be so much more fun. No wonder Dora came out to play. She's probably been bored out—"

With a flick of his tail, he knocked Bacchus to the floor.

"Gods damn it Alphonse!"

"Shut up Bach."

He ignored the whine of his friend and kept his focus trained on Dora as she continued to sashay her sexy ass away from him. Her long, blood-red hair swished across her back with each step.

She paused at one of the overflowing tables and looked over her shoulder at him.

"Leave him alone Alphonse. It isn't his fault you don't want me," she said before grabbing a bottle of wine from the tabletop.

She took a deep swig of the liquid before swinging the container between her fingers, and continuing her saunter across the room.

Alphonse stared after her in disbelief.

Not want her?

He *ached* for her. Even now his instincts warred with the need to get her out of the hall, against the need to throw her to the ground, wrap her thick thighs around his hips and fuck her into submission.

Alphonse continued staring after Dora, perplexed at her behavior. She stopped in front of a lower nightmare demon, raised her arms over her head, and began to dance. The curling tips of her hair slid across her lower back and upper swells of her breasts in taunting swirls.

Bite me.

Her body shouted the words at him even as she remained a silent enigma. He wondered if she realized how badly he wanted to do just that—bite and nip at her delicate skin while she writhed beneath him, her pussy stretched full with his dick. The fantasy of branding her all over with his mouth and cock, was a constant distraction for him.

Even now, it was enough to make him pause and stare at her undulating body instead of grabbing her and taking her away from the hall full of beings eager to have a taste of hope.

"I never figured Dora for much of a party animal, but she seems to be enjoying herself," Bacchus said.

"You're sure she's had nothing tainted?" Alphonse asked.

"On my word."

"That isn't worth much."

"Maybe, but I know my wine and substances well, and I know how you feel about her. Every jug and chalice here is enchanted to ensure she feels no effects of my potions. She may as well be drinking water."

"Then all of that—"

He waved his hand in Dora's direction.

"That's all her my friend. Every raunchy bit."

His already hardened cock twitched at that revelation. Perhaps it was time to test Dora's boundaries after all. Unpinning Bacchus from the floor, he approached Dora. By the end of the night he would have his answer.

three

ora held back tears as she brought the wine bottle to her lips and gulped.

Stupid.

She'd offered herself on a proverbial silver platter to the idiot demon and he'd stared at her as if she was crazy. When she'd turned to see the look of lust and anger stamped across Alphonse's face, she'd felt a moment of triumph. She'd wanted to pounce on him the moment she saw him but he'd treated her like some misbehaving child.

Fuck it.

She refused to continue pining after someone who didn't want her.

Shoving down her hurt, she firmed her lips, and scanned the opulent room for a distraction. She stepped in front of a dark haired demon sitting on a mound of pillows. A woman was impaled on his lap, her hips moving in a slow rocking motion. His fingers gripped the globes of the woman's butt, encouraging her languid movements.

Wanting to prove to herself and Alphonse that his reaction didn't matter, she began to dance in front of the intoxicated demon.

The tableau was one of many occurring around the room. With Alphonse's presence, the crowd had sobered slightly, but not enough to end their wicked indulgences.

The demon stared up at Dora. His eyes were glazed with lust, and Dora wondered if he even recognized his surroundings.

Leaning down, she let her breasts swing just inches from his nose. The demon's gaze followed the motion as if hypnotized and Dora's lips curled up in a bitter smile. His hands tightened on the other woman's hips and began to move them faster.

At least someone finds me sexy.

She began to sway her hips in tempo to the demon's thrusts, encouraging him to find his release with the woman gyrating on his lap.

Someone should get satisfaction tonight.

The derisive thought slid through her head, just before she was yanked backward. The wine bottle slipped from her fingers to the floor, and with a yelp, she dropped her hands down to the thick band circling her waist. Looking down she saw smooth gold scales.

Her breath stilled at the sight of the metallic hue, before tumbling from her throat in a clumsy sigh.

Alphonse.

His long tail embraced her, constricting around her, and drawing her closer. It was much stronger than she anticipated, its thick muscles lifting her from the ground, causing her feet to dangle in the air. The moment her back hit against his hard chest, a shudder ran through her body.

Rough hands rested on her shoulders, fingers pressing into her skin. He held her still as his tail pulled her tight. She bit her lower lip at the sensation. She had his hands on her at last.

Her eyes fluttered closed to savor the feel of him for a moment. She let it soak into her psyche, drowning her senses before she firmed her lips and began to struggle against his hold.

"You think I don't want you?"

He growled the words at her, his hot breath puffing against her neck. Dora stifled a moan. She wanted his lips to move closer. She'd spent so many nights fantasizing about how his lips would feel if he sucked along her flesh. Having him so close now felt like torture. She wanted to snuggle against him, and be engulfed in his heat, but her anger kept her spine straight and rigid.

It took her acting out one of her wildest fantasies to drive him into action. She didn't care if it made her fickle. The fact that she had to push him into touch her grated, but the feel of his hard cock nudging against her lower back enticed her into goading him further.

"You treat me like a child," she said.

"I can sincerely say that I've never considered you a child."

He pulled her hips snug against his letting her feel his hardness. She wrapped her fingers around his tail and held back a gasp at the smoothness of the scales. They were soft and warm to her touch.

"But tonight you seem intent on behaving like one, and the idea of spanking you does hold a certain appeal," he continued.

She blew out a breath and turned her head to look at him. His golden gaze shone with mirth and she frowned.

"I'm *naked* Alphonse."

"I have noticed that fact."

"I'm also not in the mood to be manhandled."

"And yet you walked bare-assed into this hall surrounded by strangers."

"I walked into a hall surrounded by beings honest enough to indulge in their needs."

Muscle tightened around her and she smiled. How hard would she have to push before he snapped?

"And if they chose to indulge with you?"

His fingers dug into her hips and she decided to give him one concession.

"Bacchus is your friend. I knew he wouldn't let anything happen to me."

"You trust too easily."

She sighed.

"And you don't trust at all."

He nuzzled his face into her neck and inhaled.

"You have more of my trust than anyone ever has," he said.

His whispered admission scoured her. She moved her hands to his forearms and dug her nails into his ridged flesh. The urge to melt against him and pet him into calmness ricocheted through her.

"Then why keep me away?"

"You don't feel far right now."

"You push me away every time I want to get close. Every time I need you the most," she said.

A low growl rumbled from his chest, caressing her back.

"You're mine. I would never abandon you."

"You leave me each time you touch me. You make me burn then walk away."

He released a harsh breath.

"I don't want you tainted by my...tastes."

"Alphonse..."

Her lips felt dry and a sudden burst of shyness overcame her.

"I want to please you—and I have needs as well."

She felt him stiffen behind her and begin to withdraw.

"Wait!"

Curling her hands harder along his arms she leaned into him.

"I'm not afraid of your needs," she said. "I know you

would never hurt me."

He sighed.

"It's not a matter of me hurting you, love. It's a matter of me scaring you off."

Knowing she would need to confess her own desires before he believed her, took another leap of faith.

"I've heard stories about you," she said, "of the things you like to do."

He stared down at her with a grim look on his face.

"I would never force that on you—"

"I know," she said interrupting him, "I've never experienced any of that."

She paused to gauge his reaction, but his face remained frozen in a harsh mask.

"But I'd like to," she said.

He flinched, the rigid facade of his features shifting.

"What are you saying?" he asked, his words strained and measured.

She took another deep breath and offered him the power to crush and save her all at once.

"I want you to show me what it's like to sin."

Four

Alphonse's world shattered and reformed in an instant. Dora's words bounced around in his mind—the innocent statement sending heat flashing through his body, forging his already hardened cock to steel.

"...Show me what it's like to sin."

An image of every decadent fantasy he had of Dora blazed through his brain, quickening his breath. Her mouth open and ready to take his cock.

"...Show me what it's like to sin."

Her legs spread wide and back arched as he licked at her wet pussy. With a groan, he unwound his tail from her torso and turned her body to face him.

"...Show me what it's like to sin."

Her body melted against him. Her soft breasts molded to his chest as her hips tilted upwards and settled into the cradle of his pelvis. The movements triggered the flash of an image across his mind—her ass raised in the air as he fucked her from behind.

"...Show me what it's like to sin."

He wrapped her in his arms, pulling her close and tangling his hands in her hair.

"I can't—"

He couldn't finish his denial. Her mouth parted and her perfect pink tongue peeked out to slick across her plump lips.

"Please," she whispered.

With a groan, he covered her lips with his, stealing her breath and sealing his fate at the same time. She'd ruined him. Whatever happened next would be her choice and his downfall.

He plunged his tongue deep, drowning in her taste. In a burst of energy, he transported them from the hall, whipping his power around to shield them from their audience.

The moment they reached his chambers, he pushed her against a wall.

She moaned against him, wrapping her legs around his waist. He felt her heat at the apex of her thighs through his leathers and bucked at the barrier between them. He wanted her flesh against his. He needed to coat her in the same mad frenzy she'd dipped him into.

Lifting his head, he released her mouth and stared down at her.

She looked up at him with lust glazed eyes, but that

wasn't enough for him. She'd driven him to the brink of madness and he needed her right at that same burning ledge with him.

Pushing her thighs down, he forced her to unlock her hold. Her legs slid from is waist and settled on the floor. He took a step back from her, immediately missing her heat, but relishing her whimper of distress.

"Don't worry love. I don't plan on going anywhere," he said.

Reaching for the ties at his forearms, he began to undress, letting each item of clothing drop to the ground as he held her gaze. He didn't rush his movements. He wanted her to get used to his body, to memorize the tools he planned on using to make her beg.

He toed off his boots and kicked them aside before dropping his hands to the laces of his trousers. He didn't hesitate to peel them back and display his hardness to her.

Grabbing his shaft, he stroked himself and watched as Dora licked her lips. She lifted her hand and reached for him, her long fingers caressing his cock before he stopped her movements.

Releasing his shaft, he pressed his hands to her shoulders and spun her around. Her soft ass provided a perfect pillow and he couldn't resist grinding against her. The temptation to bend her forward and make her rest her palms against the wall as he thrust into her was blinding, but he had another scenario in mind.

Her declaration from earlier still burned him.

"I don't recall you staking a claim, Alphonse."

She'd taunted him with those words and he planned on showing her exactly who she belonged to.

Pulling her tight against him, he walked backwards to his bed, allowing himself the luxury of palming her breasts as he moved.

"You chose to participate in Bacchus's festivities. Since you seem so eager to put yourself on display. Perhaps I should indulge you," he said.

Clenching his jaw, he scrapped his nails across her nipples, enjoying her gasp of pleasure. She belonged to him, and he intended to leave her with no doubt of that. He made his decision quickly. Dora chose a public forum to demand her pleasure, in return he would grant her what she demanded in the same manner.

Opening a mental link to his top guard, he sent out a message and grinned at the immediate response. Dora's initiation to his brand of pleasure would begin soon. Changing his course, he propelled them both to his favorite wing-backed chair. Sitting down he muffled a curse as her behind settled against him, the firm globes cupping his cock.

"I knew you would feel amazing against me," he said, "All this glorious skin, so soft and hot to the touch."

He ran his hands down her stomach, kneading her flesh before sliding down to her thighs and spreading them wide. He hooked his feet around hers and held her open.

"Nothing has stopped you before," she said.

"You're wrong. I had my reasons for denying us both."

"Foolish ones."

"Perhaps..."

His voice trailed as he sensed a shift in the air. Three bodies appeared before them, their images translucent and waving. Dora froze against him and his smile widen.

His personal guard had arrived.

"What is this?" she asked

She squirmed against him and tried to pull away. He chuckled at her confusion, tightened his hold and continued to caress her flesh. His little demon was about to have her darkest wishes fulfilled. All on his terms of course.

In a matter of seconds, the entities solidified, their ethereal essence forming muscles and sinew—two males and one female. They stood naked in front of him and Dora. The male's gazes drifted down her body and their cocks twitched and hardened, while the female's attention lingered on Dora's pussy. Alphonse watched Dora's nipples pebble in response.

This is going to be an enlightening night.

"Meet Michael, James and Shanna, your personal guard."

Dora's brows and lips dipped down into a tight frown.

"You mean my shadows," she said.

"*Guard*," he repeated, "They watch over you and keep

you safe when I'm not around. I have a lot of enemies, and I protect what's mine."

"There you go again, making assumptions," she said. "I belong to no one. Especially not to someone who refuses to take what I offer freely."

He laughed at her bravado.

"You've belonged to me since the moment you put your lovely hand into mine and didn't run. I've played nice with you Dora. Tonight we'll see if you can handle my bad."

He snaked his tail around her midsection before letting the length glide along her thigh. He let it rest and curl up along her knee, and watched goosebumps flush across her skin.

"What are you playing at Alphonse?"

"You decided to display your body to the spectators at Bach's feast. We'll see how far you're willing to go now," he said.

He'd chosen the trio as her guard because they worked well as a unit and he trusted them without question. Tonight, he summoned them for a different reason--they also enjoyed playing the same games he liked.

He shifted his legs wider, displaying Dora's pussy completely to the soldiers. The men began to stroke themselves and the woman reached her hands up and began to pinch her nipples. His own cock hardened further as he thought of the show he had planned. He snaked his tail farther down the side of her leg before curling it under her knee and raising it up to rest against her pussy.

Dora hissed out a breath, and her legs jerked against his. He glided between her labia stroking her for a moment, letting her arousal soak his appendage.

"I can't wait to explore you love. To fill you up in all the places you burn," he said.

"Promises, promises," she said as she rocked against him.

He flicked his tail back and smacked her pussy, making sure to tap at her clit. She yelped then moaned as he began to rub her there again to soothe the small pain.

"Look at how wet you are here, so slippery and ready to be fucked."

She glanced down her body and groaned again. The sound of her wetness filled the air and he had to grit his teeth. He wanted nothing more than to plunge into her, to be wrapped in her hot pussy as he pounded into her, but she'd issued a challenge he had every intention of meeting. With one more stroke he slid the tip of his tail across her rigid clit down to her slick opening. He penetrated her a few inches then withdrew.

He cursed at her tightness trying not to think of how close she'd feel on his cock.

Throwing her head back against his shoulder, she bit her lips and continued to pant.

"Do your worst," she said.

Her breathy taunt prickled his skin.

"Be careful what you wish for love."

Focusing on the soldiers in front of him, he nodded at the female guard.

"Shanna," he said.

"Eat."

The female groaned and knelt between their spreads legs. Placed her hands on Dora's thighs, she buried her face in Dora's pussy. Dora arched her back against him— her shriek ringing through the chamber. Liquid heat seeped from her pussy onto him as Shanna's tongue grazed his tail and licked at her slit.

"That's it. Let Shanna taste how much you want to be bad," he whispered to her.

Dora groaned and writhed in response. His cock throbbed against her ass, her undulations a temptation difficult to resist. Pumping his hips against her, he cupped both her breasts in his hands and presented them to the two males. He stroked her nipples as they watched.

"Alphonse."

Dora whispered his name and a stab of satisfaction pierced through him. Even with others present, she called out only to him.

"Don't worry darling. I'll take good care of you," he said. "Do you like Shanna's tongue? Do you like how she can't get enough of you?"

"Yes."

He pinched her nipples and let his sharp nails scrape across her soft skin.

"Look at them. They all want you."

He slid his tail into her deeper and moaned as her inner muscles gripped him. The need to lift her and drive her down hard onto his cock was overwhelming. But he needed to know how far she could go. How naughty was his little hope demon capable of being?

"They want to fuck you as badly as I do," he said, loving the way she trembled and jerked against him. "I don't give away my toys, but I don't mind sharing...at least for a little while."

Squeezing her breasts tighter he nodded to the two men. They came to stand on either side of him, each one licking their lips.

"Suck."

The moment the men's mouths latched on to her breasts, Dora exploded. She bucked on top of him, her hot pussy gripping his tail as she came.

She threw her head against his shoulder, her neck straining as screams ripped up her throat.

Beautiful.

Her wails filled the room, but Alphonse didn't relent.

"*Hmmm.* Let's see how quickly you can do that again."

"Alphonse please."

"What's that love?"

"More. I need—"

Her words died on a groan.

Fuck.

He nuzzled the side of her neck and breathed in deep, biting back his own grunt.

"Don't worry love. I'll make sure you get all the sinning you crave," he said.

"Shanna, show Dora how much you enjoyed her taste."

The woman let out a deep moan and Dora shuddered against him. Shanna eased back on her haunches before leaning her weight back on one hand and spreading her thighs wide. With her other hand Shanna spread her pussy lips open, displaying the glistening wetness there.

"Look what you did to her love. Look how one little taste of you made her so wet."

Dora whimpered and rocked harder against him, forcing his tail deeper into her hot sheath. Not wanting her to control the pleasure, he withdrew a few inches, making sure she received short, shallow thrusts.

"I think she wants some more. Too bad I don't believe in over-sharing."

With a chuckle he gave another command.

"James, I think Shanna needs something else in her mouth."

The warrior pulled away from Dora's breast and smiled. He stepped over to Shanna while stroking his cock. The thick organ strained in the man's hand, its bulbous tip already dripping with clear fluid.

Dora began to tremble against him again, her pussy dripping rivulets down his skin.

Shanna rolled to her hands and knees. On all fours, she stuck out her tongue and licked James from root to tip. The man let out a hiss and switched his hands to Shanna's cheeks. After another long lick, Shanna wrapped her lips around his cock, hallowing her cheeks and sucking him deep into her mouth.

"Watch carefully love," Alphonse said, murmuring the words against Dora's ear.

"Look at how she gobbles him up. She wants every last inch of him in her mouth," he whispered. "That will be us soon. You taking everything I can give you. Do you want that?"

"Alphonse..."

"I can't wait to do the same with you. I want to have your gorgeous lips wrapped around my cock. Would you like that? My cum filling your throat?"

"Yes!"

Dora's head rolled from side to side, but her hooded gaze remained on the scene before her. She was close again, he could feel it. Her pussy was gripping him tight and her movements were becoming erratic.

His little innocent was ready to come all over him again, aroused as much by his words as the wicked scene he created.

"Michael. I think Shanna needs a little relief. Be a

gentlemen and help her out will you."

The guard to his left grunted as he released Dora's other breast and moved towards Shanna. Stepping behind her, he knelt and grabbed the woman's hips. He rubbed his cock at the Shanna's entrance, the motion making slick wet sounds fill the room.

"Please."

Dora's plea sounded thin and strained.

"Don't worry love. Anticipation is half the fun."

He slipped his tail from her pussy and wound it up her torso to curl around her breasts. She whimpered in protest and began to thrash in his arms.

Dropping his hands down to her hips he held her still. The tip of his tail whipped from one breast to the other, gliding across her nipples.

"*Watch*," he said.

Shanna was groaning against James's dick now as she swiveled her hips against Michael's cock. The warrior held himself a breadth away, teasing Shanna with shallow strokes.

Alphonse moved a hand down to Dora's pussy, sliding two fingers between her labia. He shuddered at the feel of her. She was so hot, she almost burned to the touch. Scissoring his fingers, her trapped her clit and began to glide his hand up and down, curving along her mons.

"Anticipation gives you a moment to appreciate what's about to come. To savor the moment of relief," he murmured against the skin of her neck, before letting his teeth graze the sensitive flesh.

"It's torture," she said.

"The best kind. I can't wait to fill your pussy—to pound some submission into you."

Releasing her clit, he gripped her hips, lifted her from his lap and positioned his cock at her entrance. Letting at a loud groan, he hissed out a breath at the feel of her pussy kissing the head of his cock.

Her heat and slick arousal dripped onto him, coating his cock in a wicked promise.

"Michael."

His single command propelled the other man into action. Pulling back, Michael slammed his cock into Shanna, causing her to moan around James's cock.

In the same motion, Alphonse sank Dora onto his hard shaft.

Fuck.

He blinked against the pleasure rolling through him. Being inside her was more than he dreamed. Her pussy gripped and pulsed around him, attempting to milk his cock of everything he had.

"*Watch.*"

He growled the single word and held her tight. They were both breathing heavy, gazes trained on the trio in front of them.

Each time Michael thrust forward, Shanna was forced to

swallow more of James's cock. James grabbed the woman's head and held her still as he fucked her face, timing his thrusts to Michael's.

"Alphonse please!"

"You're almost ready, love. I just have one last question for you."

Alphonse reached between her legs again and played with her clit while his other arm held her down. He wanted her still, her pussy drowning his cock until he was ready to relieve them both.

He constricted his tail around her breasts, squeezing them together as he played with her clit.

"Who do you belong to?"

A deep moan rumbled from her chest before she shouted her response.

"You! I belong to you!"

"Exactly."

With a guttural growl he canted his hips back and thrust into her. They both shouted at the first thrust. He pounded into her, charging through her wetness and sinking deep in rapid strokes.

She screamed and bowed against him. Her pussy clamped down on him, cinching his cock like a vise. She came with a sob, a fresh flood of her cum dripping down his cock, but still he didn't stop. He wanted to wring her dry, fill her with cum and then start all over again.

Dora insisted on being sullied, and he intended on

fulfilling every dirty fantasy.

Her head lulled to the side, and she blinked lust-dazed eyes at him. The look fueled his ardor, making him increase his thrusts and strokes. She would be bruised in the morning, and that thought wasn't enough to make him slow his movements or loosen his hold.

He needed to drum the rhythm of his cock into her, create a beat that her body would always crave. Pulling back and ramming hard into her, he gritted his teeth.

Her lips moved in a soft murmur. Leaning his head down he strained to hear. Even if she begged him to stop, he didn't think he could. Her pussy was heaven, and he didn't plan on ever giving it up.

Her lips moved again, and this time he heard her request. Voice hoarse from screaming, she whispered a single word.

"More."

His cock twitched at the scratchy quality of her voice. She'd screamed her throat raw and all he wanted to do was make her do it again. Groaning against her skin he bucked against her as the first streams of cum jerked from his body.

Fuck.

She held his gaze as her pussy trembled around him again, the muscles milking him, accepting every drop of his essence he had to offer. Her eyes shimmered and skin glowed—her mouth puffy from nibbling on her lips. Sweat slicked down her body converging at her crotch where it mingled with her cum and his.

Feeling himself begin to harden again at the sight, his only thought was that he'd been right—Dora looked beautiful dripping in sin.

Five

ora drifted on a hot dream.

She was so full. Her pussy felt stretched and her body flushed in heat.

"I'm not done with you yet."

She shivered at the husky voice whispering through her mind.

Alphonse.

"Hmm."

Strong arms lifted her and the fullness disappeared. She murmured in protest before dropping a hand down to her pussy to stroke the bundle of nerves above her slit.

"Soon love."

She smiled to herself. She was dreaming again. It was the only explanation for the euphoric feel in her limbs and the sound of Alphonse's voice.

Leaving one hand between her thighs, she curled the other up to her right breast and began to play with her nipple. With a sigh, she recalled her dream. It had been so vivid and decadent. Her pussy throbbed as if she had received a pounding.

A soft chuckle filled her ears.

"I don't mind if you have a head start, but give me a moment to get you to bed."

She stilled and her eyes popped open at the words spoken so close.

With a gasp she took in her surroundings. Dark-granite floors gleamed in the dim light leading up to white onyx walls. Dark wooden furniture was spread across the space with a large four poster bed placed high on at the far side of the room.

Alphonse.

This was no dream—it was all real. Inhaling deep, she pulled in spicy scent. His strong arms surrounded her as he carried her through the room. She gulped as they approached the bed, her mind replaying the acts she'd experienced before drifting to sleep. Heat rushed to her cheeks as she turned her head to look over his shoulder, searching for the trio of guards.

"They're gone now," Alphonse said.

She let out a small sigh of relief. She'd enjoyed the experience, but wanted to have Alphonse to herself. Her heart sped up as she let that reality sink in. His strong arms tightened around her.

"Nothing to say?" he asked.

Her hand tightened on her pussy, arousal flooding her

at the feel of his voice vibrating through his chest and caressing her side.

Tilting her head, her gaze caught his and any flippant response she had ready died at the heat burning in his stare. Licking her lips, she nodded and said the only words her mind and body could muster.

"More please."

With a gruff curse he dropped her to the bed. Her view tilted and she bounced once before settling down into the plush, soft surface. Lifting herself up on her elbows, she looked up at him, taking in every delicious inch of him.

Thick muscles flexed and bunched beneath his golden skin. Sweat dripped down his chest, highlighting the sprinkle of blond hair trailing down his abdomen to his crotch. It was a delicious arrow to the hard cock that had given her such pleasure. His shaft strained up from between his legs, the thick-rounded tip reaching his navel. The rigid organ glistened in the light, covered in their mingled cum.

Her mouth went dry wondering how their combined flavors would taste. As if knowing her thoughts, he reached down and stroked himself.

"You haven't had enough?" he asked.

"Never."

Her gaze trailed back up his body to his face. Her blood buzzed at the sight of the ruddy flush slashed across his cheeks.

"When will you realize that I need all of you?"

His cheek ticked, the taut skin rippling over his scar. She frowned at the telling motion. Did he really continue to doubt her? Her body still tingled from their mating, and already hungered for more. How could he believe she wouldn't still want him?

"If I left your chambers right now, would you come after me?"

The muscles on his cheek jumped again and he clenched his jaw.

"I already told you. You're mine. I'm not letting you go."

"Then what would you do with me? Hold my hand and kiss my cheek for eternity?"

A small smile quirked his lips.

"Eternity? I'm glad you understand my way of thinking."

She rolled her eyes before smirking up at him.

"Do you honestly think you can stomp around claiming I'm yours without me wanting to do the same?" she asked. "Alphonse, *you've* been *mine* since the day you took my hand and looked at me like I was dessert and you wanted to lick me up."

She let her legs fall open, letting him see how wet and swollen she was. His curse filled the space. His cocked swelled larger, the tip crowning with a small pearl of fluid.

"I want to do more than that," he said.

"And I want you to do it all," she said.

He let out another terse curse and his body covered hers a moment later. She clutched his shoulders as his lips found hers. His taste exploded across her mouth as his tongue twined with hers. She spread her legs wide, trapping his hips between her legs as she ground her wetness against him.

This is what she craved. Alphonse lost in passion—not afraid to show her his worst. Watching her three guards had been a decadent treat—a voyeuristic fantasy—but *this* was what she wanted; Alphonse as adrift in arousal as she was.

The tip of his penis slipped into her stretching her entrance wide. She canted her hips, desperate to take him deeper, but he controlled her too well.

He held her hips firm while his mouth commanded hers, his tongue delving deep and stroking hers the way she wanted his cock to dominate her pussy.

Her chest burned with the need to breathe, but she pushed the discomfort aside for more of his spicy flavor. When he lifted his head, she whimpered at the loss even as her lungs spasmed, desperate for air.

He dipped his head to the crook of her neck, his teeth grazing the sensitive juncture above her collarbone.

"Tell me to stop."

He growled the words against her skin. She smiled and attempted to rock her hips again.

"No," she said.

His rumble vibrated through her, prickling her already

heightened senses. In a swift shift of motion, he thrust his hips forward, plunging his cock into her.

She gasped at the fullness of having him so deep, then moaned as she felt him throb inside her.

He lifted his head snaring her gaze with his. His eyes were a wild swirl of silver and she wanted to laugh out in triumph.

"I can't be gentle. Not this time," he said.

"I don't want you to be."

With a growl he flexed his hips back and withdrew from her before returning in a hard thrust. He repeated the movements setting a rough rhythm accentuated by the sound of slapping wet flesh and guttural grunts.

She tightened around him, her body wanting to pull him in deeper, her pussy flowing to create more slippery friction.

He bent and captured one of her stiffened nipples in his mouth. Shrieking beneath him, she arched her back. His rough tongue stroked the pebbled flesh before his strong teeth nipped it, causing a bite of pain before spreading into pleasure.

Her pussy creamed around him, liquid heat flowing down his cock and pooling at the crack of her ass. In moments he reduced her to a pile of pulsing flesh, melting and begging for more. She'd been so wrong in her plot. She'd wanted him to break, to reveal his true self, instead he'd stolen her soul, shattered *her* control.

Nothing prepared her for his all-consuming possession of her.

He released her nipple and moved to the next one, his tongue leaving a hot trail between the valley of her breasts. Each suck, lick, and bite was in tune to his rough strokes.

She couldn't think past his next thrust, couldn't breathe without his body pounding into hers.

Shifting up he sat back on his knees. The new angle drove him farther into her depths. He dug his fingers into her hips, lifting her to him. She would be sore in the morning and didn't care. All that mattered was the next glide of his flesh against hers.

As if understanding her need for more contact, Alphonse whipped his tail forward—sliding up her torso. The soft scales of the silk appendage set off goosebumps in their wake.

Her mind splintered. How could she ever go back to tame caresses and gentle touches? She needed this raw hunger, this explosive claiming.

"I've imagined every way to take you, but nothing compares to this," he said.

He panted out the words, each one leaving his mouth with a tortured grunt. His tail wrapped around her swollen breasts, squeezing them in a wicked embrace.

Her nipples felt on fire, throbbing at the restriction of blood. The tingling pressure sent more fluid surging through to her core.

"Alphonse, please!"

His gaze drifted down her body and settled on her pussy.

"Beautiful," he whispered, "I knew you'd be gorgeous all stretched out and wet on my cock."

His tempo increased, pushing her to the brink. It was too much.

He pounded into her, each forward stroke tapping at her clitoris in a maddening beat. His tail squeezed her breasts tighter, the tip flicking between the two peaks to slap at her nipples.

He glanced back up at her.

"This is what I want Dora, you begging to be filled. Demanding that I fuck you as long and as hard as I want."

She whimpered at the truth and promise in his words.

Yes.

She was so close, her release hovering on the precipice of his control. In a swift movement his tail released her breasts. The blood rushed to her skin spreading needle pinpricks across her skin and pushing her over the edge. She convulsed around him, her mouth opened wide on a scream.

Writhing, she jerked her hips against him needing to pull him in deeper—to cover him in her essence and bathe in his.

He stiffened above her, his face going taut. With a shout he pulsed inside of her, his cum spurting hot and hard into her pussy. Each burst set off aftershocks in her core, making her inner muscles contract and flutter.

She strained against him, not wanting the connection between their bodies to end. With a final shudder, he collapsed over her, landing on his forearms.

Their breath mingled, both of them trying to fill their lungs with air and slow the rapid pace of their heart beats. She wrapped her hands around his waist and tugged him down against her chest. His heart hammered against her breasts and she smiled. His eyelids drooped low in a satisfied blink before he dropped his head down for a kiss.

This was a slow mingling of the lips, a languid caress of tongues that melted her bones and sped her heart up once more.

He pressed his body down on hers and rolled them both to their sides. She let out a soft squeak against his mouth. His cock slipped from her body, the loss of it making her inner muscles clench in longing.

With a sigh she hooked a leg over his outer thigh. He lifted his head and stared down at her, his silver eyes filled with satisfaction.

"Remind me again why we didn't do this sooner?" she asked.

"Because, I'm a fool," he said.

She smirked and rested her head against his chest.

"As long as we're in agreement," she said.

He chuckled.

Silence settled between them. His big hand stroked her back and as she became lost in her own thoughts. There had been a few moments when she feared he'd turn her away, but she was finally in his arms. He'd taken her pleasure to new heights. Her body still tingled and craved more. Fatigue tugged at her but, if he reached for her, she would spread her legs and welcome his passion again.

Knowing that he no longer hid his true self from her she confessed her own secret to him.

"I love you," she whispered.

He stiffened beside her and remained silent. As the moments ticked by her eyes filled with hot-unshed tears.

Gods damn it!

Had she really been such an idiot? Did his feelings only stop at affection and lust? She began to pull away, but his grip held her down.

"Dora look at me."

Her lips trembled at his command, and she shook her head in denial.

With a sigh he placed his thumb beneath her chin and tilted her head back, forcing her to look at him.

"Only one thing has ever scared me," he said.

He smoothed her hair back from her face and held her head between his large hands.

"You turning away from me, in either fear or disgust. That if I revealed how much I wanted you, that you would walk away," he said.

His eyes shone with so much emotion her breath clogged in her throat.

"I've wanted you from the moment I first laid eyes on you, but I've loved you from the first moment you blinked your pretty eyes at me and I realized I never wanted you to stop."

Her mouth fell open at his confession.

"You love me?"

She whispered the words, afraid that any sound would disintegrate the fantasy building around her. Her heart swelled as he smiled down at her.

"Yes," he said.

"I didn't think you would want the type of pleasure I indulged in, but I was willing to give it up to keep you."

"Did you ever plan on making love to me?"

He leaned down and touched his forehead to hers.

"I wanted to wait until I knew I could control myself. I didn't want to hurt you. Now I wonder what would have happened if I told you that first day how much I wanted to throw you to the ground and ravish you."

"Silly demon," she said.

She stretched up her arms and looped them around his neck, pressing her breasts into his chest.

"My answer will always be the same," she said.

"And what's that?" he asked, the corners of his eyes crinkling.

She smiled against his lips before replying.

"More please."

His chest rumbled against hers as his laughter filled the room.

"And I'll always be happy to oblige," he said before capturing her lips with his. "Always."

The End

Guilt's

PLEASURE

"He was now in that state of fire that she loved. She wanted to be burnt."

—*Anaïs Nin, Delta of Venus*

One

*O*n *your knees.*

With an anguished cry, Morgan jerked awake. For a moment she lay there, her heart racing. After a few strangled breaths, she untangled herself from her damp sheets, before sitting up and leaving her bed. Running her hands through her long curling hair she began to pace her bedchamber. Sweat marked her brow and the soft skin between her breasts and shoulder blades. Her wings flexed and twitched behind her, expanding out to their full length before closing in and dropping down her back. The mild discomfort didn't compare to the hunger shaking through her body.

The dreams were becoming more frequent.

Clenching her fists at her sides she held back a shiver and resisted the urge to stroke her hands down her abdomen and find some relief. Each night her dreams became more detailed, and each night she woke in an intense state of need.

Images of her on her knees allowing her body to be used

in wicked abandon flashed through her mind. The dreams were a taunt—manifestations of desires she was unable to act on.

At first she'd sought self-satisfaction through masturbation, but after a few days that hadn't been enough. Only one person could relieve the burn licking its way through her body—and he hated her.

Dax.

A shiver zipped down her body at the thought of him. With pale skin, long dark-red hair and coal-black eyes, some would call him handsome, but he had a coldness about him that made most look away before they could get a closer look. Upon closer inspection, they would find a strong stubborn jaw, full lush lips and eyes so dark they were like endless pools to drown in. His cool calm was in direct contrast to the hot cloak of power draped around him. As a fire demon, and member of Vinghel's high guard, Dax was not a demon to be taken lightly. His frigid demeanor hid immense power that he harvested with ruthless control.

Until recently, she'd never seen him raise his voice in anger or make a single move that wasn't deliberate or calculated.

"Leave!"

Closing her eyes, she recalled the look of fury on his face when she'd told him about Sigmund's betrayal.

Hate, loathe, despise.

Those words were too tame to describe the look on Dax's face that day. The memory still caused an ache in her chest. They'd once been friends, but her connection with Sigmund and hand in his death had severed that tie. At least in Dax's eyes. Yet, knowing his feelings didn't prevent her from dreaming about him.

The recollection of her latest dream chased a shudder down her body, causing her to clench her thighs tight. Until she convinced him to forgive her, she would find no true relief.

While Dax harbored hatred, she suffered from mounds of guilt coupled with a yearning to be close to him.

For Morgan, his hatred only made the patchwork of their relationship more complex.

As reasons for hating her went, he had a pretty good one. Sigmund, Dax's best friend was dead—and she'd killed him. Worse still, was the fact that she harbored more remorse for keeping the killing a secret from Dax, than taking Sigmund's life. Her father, Vinghel himself, had charged her with the mission to investigate Sigmund, and snuff out the uprising the lower demon had been planning.

She'd spent her entire life being a dutiful daughter. Being born into the ruling family of Hell, the house of Vinghel, she was taught the importance of honor. When the time came for her to take on a designation of power, she followed her sisters and took on the mantle of a furiae with pride.

Furiaes were vengeance demons, given the power to seek out retribution. She loved what she did. She'd seen what happened when wrongs went unpunished, and wanted to be a force of good in the universe.

When she'd first learned of Sigmund's treachery, she didn't hesitate to move forward with plans to catch him and any others involved in his machinations. When her father suggested they keep the mission secret from Dax, she'd agreed. A part of her had known her relationship with Dax would be a casualty, but she'd proceeded anyway.

Now she was left with the remnants of his rage. His animosity wore on her—peeling back the thin layers of control left on her psyche.

Patience.

She chuckled at her internal admonishment. The time for patience was past. It was the ultimate irony— that the moment she'd realized she loved Dax was the moment she'd lost him.

Defeat didn't sit well with her. She'd never had to wrestle with the feeling of crushing loss before. She didn't like it and refused to accept it as her future. If she had any hope of convincing Dax of the truth and gaining any measure of his affection back, she had to stay focused and come up with a plan.

Several ideas came to mind, but she dismissed each one as they came. Dax was too intelligent to be fooled by a simple ruse. He was both smart and lethal, a combination that she'd always found fascinating.

He had a remarkable skill for making weapons. His powers as a fire demon allowed him to forge metals and other elements into beautiful objects of art or destruction. He'd told her once that he considered them all the same.

"Whether I make something to kill or inspire, it holds some essence of beauty to it."

Seeing the things he'd created in his workshop, she had to agree.

His workshop was filled with a menagerie of sculptures, weapons, chains, and other objects of both beauty and pain.

His skill had earned him the role of chief inquisitor for Vinghel's guard.

She recalled the first time she brought a prisoner to him for interrogation. She'd watched Dax bind the man to a wall before walking across the room to select his choice of torture.

After several moments of silence, she'd grown impatient.

* * *

"I understand that you have a lot of toys to choose from, but perhaps you can decide to get on with it sometime this century," she said.

He paused in his perusal to give her a sharp smile.

"I've already started," he said.

Hissing out a breath, she waited several more minutes before he chose an instrument—a heavy set of chains with large clamps on either end.

Wing cutters.

There weren't many things that made her cringe, but the metal vise known to snap the wings from winged demons, was one of them.

The prisoner began to shake as soon as Dax approached.

Morgan expected Dax to immediately strap the device to the accused demon. Instead, Dax stood in front of him and waited—the long chinks swaying from his fingers, the metal making a soft clinking sound with each swing.

Again her impatience led her to speak up.

"Dax—"

He silenced her with one glance, his strong jaw clenching in warning. She remained silent after that, holding her tongue until he was finished. She didn't have too long to wait this time. Dax raised the chains up to the man dangling in the center of the room, and grazed them along his chest.

"Do you know what these are?" he asked.

The man remained firm in his silence, but whimpered when Dax draped the heavy chains over his shoulders.

"This is the thing that stands between you, death, and an existence far worse," Dax said.

Moving behind the demon, he took the ends of the cutters and clamped each one to a muddy brown wing extending from the demon's back.

The chain trailed down the center of the demon's back.

"It's made from the strongest metal, tempered in waters from the River Styx and blessed by Vinghel himself. Can you imagine what will happen if I decided to twist this chain tight?" he asked.

Within moments the demon began to give up all the information he had. The entire transaction was fascinating to Morgan. Without marring a single inch of the demon's flesh, Dax managed to extract a full confession where others—including herself—had failed.

* * *

Morgan smiled at the memory. She should have known then, that nothing was ever as it seemed with Dax. Afterward, still stunned, she'd asked him how he'd known what to do.

"Sometimes the knowledge that someone can harm you, is more powerful and crippling than the act itself," he'd said.

Recalling his response now, triggered another memory— one that still made her cheeks flush with heat. A few weeks before she learned of Sigmund's betrayal, Dax caught her examining one of his whips and said the words that blew her world apart.

* * *

"Not everything here is meant to draw pain."

She lifted a brow at his comment.

"I'm not an idiot. I know there are some who enjoy a little pain with their pleasure," she said.

Stroking the fine leather of the whip she watched him. His face remained a stone mask, but she thought she detected a small spark light his eyes. Before she could be sure, he lowered his gaze to her hands.

"Are you one of that crowd Morgan?"

Heat skittered through her at the question.

"I don't think so."

"Don't think, or don't know?"

Her mouth went dry at his question. Licking her lips, she tried to get her skittering heart beat under control.

"I'm not sure."

A slow smile quirked his lips, before his gaze found hers again. There was no mistaking the lust sparking his eyes this time.

"Let me know when you do."

The heat in his gaze held her speechless. He reached out to her, his large hands grazing her fingers. A spear of heat lanced from that point of contact sizzling across her breasts and settling hot and needy in her pussy. Her fingers went slack from the shock of arousal. The whip fell from her hands and he caught it with a precise flip of his wrist.

The moment his skin stopped touching hers she bolted from the room. She didn't know how to process her body's reaction to a man she considered a friend, so she decided retreat was in her best interests.

* * *

Shaking her head of the memory, Morgan raised her hands to her head and rubbed at her temples.

His throaty chuckle had followed her from the chamber. She didn't know if his husky laughter was a warning or a promise, but her mind and body had ceased to care.

That was the last time she'd seen him before her father tasked her with apprehending Sigmund.

Thinking of it all now, a plan began to form in Morgan's mind. What would happen if she offered Dax a means for revenge while providing herself an opportunity to atone? He'd said perceived power held a great weight. What would happen if she offered him complete power with no illusions to the contrary?

Another shiver worked its way down her spine at the possibilities. Coming to a decision, she strode to her wardrobe, and dressed in quick movements. If she didn't act now, she wasn't sure if she'd have the confidence to do it later.

With a quick turn she strode across the room and opened the glass doors leading to her balcony. Allowing herself one final moment of self-doubt, she paused to stare up at the night sky.

In the Underworld, the sky was always a swirling mixture of shades of red and black, punctuated by streaks of blue. There was no sun, only a single aperture resembling a moon, that loomed over it all. It's location never changed. It always remained centered in the sky staring down at them all in silent assurance. Throughout the day, it blinked closed in a slow wink. The transition caused the glow of the moon to change from a golden glow, to a silver blue. The blue illuminated the night sky in a hazy blanket that always managed to calm Morgan. She kept her gaze focused on the glimmering globe and took a deep breath.

This could be her last chance to have any type of future with Dax. A part of her hoped that he took the bargain she was about to offer, while another was terrified he would. Either choice would leave her emotions exposed to the one being capable of crushing her.

Stop procrastinating.

Tilting her head back and forth and shaking her hands out at her sides to loosen her limbs, she spread her wings out behind her. With one strong leap she was over the ledge and soaring through the air.

He wouldn't appreciate her intrusion, but she'd spent her lifetime fighting for justice, it was time she did the same for her happiness.

two

Dax strode down the hall of is home towards his workshop, eager to get his hands on some tools. In the last few weeks it had become the only place he could find a distraction from the litany of guilt, shame, and throbbing lust filling his head.

Working with his metals allowed him to reset his mind. It gave him the time needed to focus and pull the veil of calm control he needed as a high chief in Vinghel's guard, back in place. The process had become more and more difficult over the past few months. Ever since he'd made *her* leave.

Morgan.

Images and memories of the sexy little vengeance demon filled his mind almost every minute. *She* was the reason he couldn't focus, *she* was the source of his sleepless nights and *she* was responsible for the endless hours of self-condemnation.

"Leave!"

He'd shouted the words at her, the last time he saw her.

No doubt, everyone assumed he grieved for the loss of his friend, Sigmund. But the truth was he raged at himself. He'd allowed emotions to get in the way of reason. His friendship with Sigmund, blinded him to the demon's evil deeds and put the lives of Vinghel and the entire ruling family of the Underworld at risk.

He couldn't risk that happening again—even if it meant giving up the only woman he'd ever wanted to claim as his own.

Seeing Morgan standing before him that night, so sad and alone tore at him. He'd wanted to pull her to him and re-assure her that she'd done the right thing, and that need angered him further. His first thoughts at that moment should have been for the welfare of Vinghel and the rest of the guard, not focused on a single woman.

The longer he'd stared at her the more enraged he became. They'd kept the investigation a secret from him. That fact burned him, the implications of it scarring him deeper than any wound he'd ever received in battle.

* * *

"I'm sorry Dax. The evidence was clear so Vinghel gave the order."

"And you obeyed like a good little vengeance demon. Why wasn't I told sooner?" he demanded.

She flinched, but looked him in the eyes.

"You were his friend, Vinghel didn't—"

He hissed in a breath and stepped forward.

"He didn't trust me to do what's right?"

Her eyes widened and she shook her head.

"No! He didn't want you to be hurt."

"Hurt?"

The single word skewered him. He was part Vinghel's high guard. He'd battled demons and other beings for centuries. His skill was almost unmatched. He didn't get hurt.

She licked her lips and nodded.

"Sigmund was your friend. You were too close..."

He couldn't follow the rest of her reply. Too close. *The two words vaulted around in head. Emotion had made him weak. His friendship had blinded him to Sigmund's true nature. Watching Morgan stand in front of him, her eyes wide and vulnerable, he snapped.*

"Get out."

He said the words in an even tone, using every ounce of will he had not

"Dax, please. You have to understand"

"Get. Out."

"I said leave!"

His shout echoed through the room. Her blood amber eyes shimmered for a moment, glistening with unshed tears. That liquid glimmer almost broke his control, but she pressed her lips into a tight line, bowed her head in a curt nod and left.

* * *

He relived that moment several hundred times a day. Morgan was one of the strongest demons in the guard and to see her struggle with her part in Sigmund's death was difficult to watch. That sheen of tears haunted him, but he maintained his resolve.

Keeping Morgan in his life put his position within Vinghel's guard at risk. She evoked emotions in him, that distracted him, made him weak. He couldn't risk Vinghel or anyone else believing that he couldn't do his job again.

Gritting his teeth against the memory, he pushed open the heavy doors to his sanctuary. The moment he stepped inside his muscles loosened.

The workshop housed all of his tools. Located on the ground floor of his home, it was well located for his work and had tall glass doors leading out to a private courtyard. Several stone workbenches were placed throughout the space, with a huge blacksmithing forge set up near the far wall.

The large room was long and narrow, allowing him to set up several workspaces. He spent so much time in the shop, that he had several comfortable chairs set near the forge where he could sit and relax whenever his mind gave him a moment of solace. Lately, he couldn't seem to find a sliver of it with thoughts of Morgan clogging his mind.

Like many of Vinghel's twelve daughters, Morgan possessed the distinct black wings of a furiae, an

Underworld maiden of justice. The dark feathers, glinted with a kaleidoscope of colors when she moved as if an iridescent rainbow sheathed each plume. Her almond shaped eyes were a soft amber that glowed red when she was angry and warmed to gold when she was happy. All of that coupled with her soft golden hued skin, made her resemble a lost jewel from an ancient treasure chest.

He shook his head as he made his way to the forge. With a flick of his hand, a surge of power leapt from his fingers and lit the embers in the large furnace, filling the thick stone chamber with a blazing fire. Another wave of his hand blew open the doors to his courtyard, allowing a slight breeze to drift through the shop. As always, when he was forced to seek refuge here late at night, he began with shaping a new piece of steel. The physical work needed to pound and force the strong metal to submission helped clear his mind.

Reaching for a chunk he'd left burning in the embers the night before, he held the piece in his hands, heating it further with his powers until it turned a bright orange-yellow color. Satisfied with the level of heat, he picked up a nearby a set of heavy tongs and a sledge hammer. Placing the metal on an anvil and holding it steady with the tongs, he lifted the hammer high and swung it down hard on the metal.

Sparks crackled through the air and he let out a grunt of satisfaction.

This he could control—the forging and shaping of metal,

even when thoughts of Morgan intruded on his peace of mind.

He was an honest man—at least to himself. Morgan began messing with his concentration way before the debacle with Sigmund. Her lethal grace and unwavering sense of justice, paired with her thick halo of long curls and golden skin played with his mind. He wanted to both challenge and protect—conquer and cherish. All things that kept him off balance and prevented him from obtaining the cold focus he needed. Every time he saw or thought of her, one thought bounced through his mind.

Mine.

Gritting his teeth, he increased the force of his movements, enjoying the feel of his muscles stretching and straining. How was he supposed keep his cool and maintain his distance when each night the need to claim Morgan, to make her burn as much as he did, drove him to the brink of madness?

Love does that to a man.

Love—he scoffed at the word. Love didn't exist in his destiny and the sooner he convinced his errant heart of that, he'd be back to normal.

As if summoned by his turmoil, the sweet scent of roasted cinnamon filled the air making his mouth water. His shoulders stiffened for a moment before he swung the sledge hammer down in a final swing.

He should have known that eventually, his tormentor

would seek him out.

A final set of sparks burst through the air as he smashed the metal between the heavy weight of the hammer and the solid anvil. Dropping the hammer to the side, he turned and placed the flattened metal back in the furnace.

He examined the glowing piece for a moment, before turning to the glass doors flanking the side of the room.

"Do you plan on hiding in the shadows all night?" he asked.

A small sigh drifted through the air. Dressed in dark green leathers that hugged her lush curves, and a long dark cloak, Morgan stepped through the open doors that led out to his terrace.

His muscles bunched and tightened when he saw her. She always had the same effect on him—a punch of lust hitting him deep, before ebbing to a low throb.

Mine.

"I didn't want to disturb you," she said.

His eyelids drooped down a moment—the split second he needed to bank the growing fire inside him.

"That time is long past, Morgan. What do you want?"

She flinched at his blunt response, but he refused to soften his voice. The quicker she left, the quicker he could breathe normally again.

"I came to offer you a bargain," she said.

He quirked his lips at her confidence. Always the strong furiae, convinced in whatever crusade she'd decided was on the side of right.

"Why would I make a bargain with you?"

"Because I'm offering you the one thing your honor won't let you have," she said.

He raised his brows at her declaration. He doubted she had any idea what he wanted or needed.

"And what's that?"

"Revenge."

"You think I crave revenge?"

"I know you do."

He dropped his gaze and turned away from her. Walking to his favorite chair by the fire, he sat and hooked his leg over the chair's arm. He glanced back at her, enjoying the flicker of irritation across her face.

"How would your bargain offer me revenge?" he asked.

She hesitated for a moment before answering.

"You're still angry about Sigmund's death," she said.

His shoulders stiffened.

"Angry doesn't even begin to describe what I feel Morgan."

She let out a deep breath.

"I know, and I wish I could change the truth, but nothing will change the facts. He betrayed all of us—"

"And you killed him for it," he said.

Her lips trembled, but her voice remained clear.

"Yes."

"Do you regret it?"

"I regret not telling you sooner."

Her answer didn't surprise him. Every act Morgan made was with conviction. She wouldn't take another's life unless she felt the act would bring justice. That knowledge didn't help quell the burn of shame stinging his heart. She should have had faith in his ability to handle Sigmund.

"How will your bargain change that?"

She licked her lips and stepped forward.

"You told me once that sometimes knowing someone can harm you is more powerful than the act itself. I'm here to offer you that power."

He stilled at her words.

"Explain."

"Sigmund was my friend too. Taking his life wasn't easy. It's left me with some measure of guilt."

"And your bargain will help cure you of that? I don't see how that would benefit me at all."

"It will help us both."

She turned from him and walked to the far wall of the chamber. Her fingertips crazed across several whips and chains hanging from hooks on the wall, her small hands looking delicate against the dark leather and cold metal. Glancing up at him, she wrapped her hands around a pair of leather cuffed shackles. Lifting them from the wall, she made her way back to him.

His blood pulsed loud against his eardrums as she

approached, her hips swaying in a gentle rhythm. She stopped in front of him and dropped to her knees. Her gaze locked on his. The determination he saw in her stare set off a warning buzz in his head. Lifting her chin, she held the shackles out to him, her voice clear and steady.

"I'm offering you one night—one night to punish me and allow me to atone."

He hissed out a breath. Why was it always so easy for this small demon to wreck him? Her words tore through his psyche and settled with sharp accuracy in his chest.

"You think I want you punished?"

Is that what she thought he wanted for her? Pain flashed across her features, before she tilted her head down, allowing her long hair to mask her face.

"Yes."

Curling his fingers into the soft leather of his chair, he stared down at her bowed head.

Why was it so easy for her to cut him so deep? He didn't want to look at her and feel anything—to be faced with his own weakness. There was a time when he dreamed about her like this, on her knees submitting to him, but now too much emotion was rolled up in the action.

He didn't *want* emotion. He wanted calm, cool, control—the return of the composed discipline over his senses he had before he met her.

Before everything.

Uncurling a hand, he reached for the restraints and lifted them from her hands. The chains settled cool and heavy in his palms. He smoothed his fingers along the soft leather of the cuffs, and watched her gaze follow the movement.

Her attention frayed the edges of his control. His grip tightened around the restraints.

Perhaps this is what he needed. The chance to purge himself of his fantasies of her while re-establishing his control. He'd have one night to rein in his emotions and flush her from his system.

"Bargain accepted," he said.

Her shoulders drooped and she sighed.

"Thank you," she said before making to stand.

"Not so fast."

Her brows scrunched down in a frown and he smiled. She'd flown into his sanctuary tonight and threw his world off it's already precarious axis. He planned to return the favor.

"I have some stipulations."

She frowned, but settled back on her knees.

"What are they?" she asked.

Dropping the shackles back to his lap, he sat back in the chair.

"They're quite simple."

He held up his hand and began ticking off his rules.

"One—when you come to me, I want you naked. Nothing drives home vulnerability like nudity, and I want you to have no doubt, that I'm the one in control of you while you're here."

She licked her lips, but gave a short nod of agreement.

"Two—and this is the most important. The moment you say 'No', it will all be over. You'll leave this place and never bother me again. Understood?"

She nodded again.

"Lastly—when you come to me, I want your absolute submission. You offered me full rights to control and I intend to take them. You owe me this."

Her agreement was slower this time. He watched the skin of her exposed arms ripple with goosebumps. She licked her lips again, her rosy tongue, slicking out before her upper teeth snagged her lower lip in a delicate nibble. His stomach clenched and he ground his teeth. It was always like this.

She'd always had the ability to tie him in knots. Her strength goaded him into pushing her limits, while her vulnerability made him want to protect her. Both qualities made him want her period. It was an annoying conundrum, that made it so difficult for him to forget her. It was why the final rule was non-negotiable. Complete control was the only way he'd get through their little pact without revealing himself.

Even now, the urge to reach forward and offer her solace was coupled with images of her thick lips wrapped around his cock.

Instead he sat back and held her troubled gaze. Her indecision was stamped clearly across her face, but after several long moments she responded.

"Alright."

He let out a slow, shallow breath. There would be no going back now. With a derisive twist of his lips, he sealed both their fates.

"Good, then we're in agreement."

She bowed her head again and reached for the clasp of her cloak.

"No!"

She stilled at his command and he smiled. Already, she was following orders well.

"You offered me one night, and this one is half over," he said, "Return tomorrow and we can begin. Be here by first moon shift."

He watched her swallow and enjoyed her discomfort. She rose to her feet and he remained sitting watching her leave. How would she react tomorrow when she realized her mistake? Only naive fools bargained with someone who had too much to lose.

three

Morgan hovered inside Dax's courtyard, taking deep calming breaths. From her location she could see the inside of Dax's workshop. He hadn't arrived yet and she was relieved. She masked her presence this time, needing the extra moments to prepare herself. Her fingers clutched at the long velvet cape cloaking her body and she nibbled at her lips.

She'd spent the hours between last night and now, facilitating between anticipation and fear. Anticipation to finally experience the acts she only allowed herself to enjoy in her dreams, and fear that Dax would see through her ruse and call an end to their bargain. There was more than her pleasure at stake tonight. It may be the last chance she had to win Dax.

"Second thoughts?"

She froze at the sound of Dax's raspy voice. Peering over her shoulder she saw him step from a shadowed corner of the yard. She swallowed against the dryness in her mouth as he came toward her. He wore dark leather pants that hugged the thick muscles of his thighs, but his chest was bare. Moonlight caressed the hard muscle of his exposed skin as he approached and Morgan fought the urge to reach for him.

Abandoning her attempt to remain invisible, she materialized fully. She should have known that she couldn't hide from him. Shaking her head as much in answer to his question, as to admonish herself, she replied.

"No. You know me better than that. I never go back on my word."

He stopped in front of her, leaving only a few inches separating them. His dark scent filled her nose. It was a heady combination of embers and vanilla. She licked her lips as his gaze traveled down her body.

"Perhaps, but it looks like you've already broken my first rule."

Heat surged through her at the reminder of her nudity beneath the cloak. She hadn't forgotten his stipulation, but preferred not to fly through the Underworld bare-assed. Raising her chin, she reached for the clasp at her throat, and let the garment drop to the ground.

He glanced down her body again, leaving a lick of heat on each inch of skin his stare touched. His features remained guarded, but a familiar flame lit his eyes.

"Follow me."

She trailed behind him as he led her inside. Both the forge and fireplace blazed with fire, but despite the warmth they provided, she couldn't keep a shiver from snaking its way down her spine.

He paused in the center of the room and turned to her. Crossing his arms over his chest, he braced his legs apart. The smooth planes of his face settled into harsh lines.

"Kneel."

She held back a groan at the command. It was so close to the orders his dream version gave her. Without hesitation, she dropped down to her knees on the floor and waited. He walked around her and paused at her back.

"Place your palms up on your knees and spread your thighs. I want you open and vulnerable at all times," he said.

Her skin warmed as she followed his command. He returned to the front and stared down at her.

"Tonight you'll learn the basics and we'll both discover your hard limits," he said.

"I've already told you. I want this. It will benefit us both," she said.

His features hardened at her response.

"Let's be honest with each other here," he said.

He bent down and grabbed her chin. His callused fingers dug into her skin. She wanted to melt into the harsh hold, but remained still. Letting out a shallow breath she waited for him to speak.

"Whatever softness you're expecting from me you won't get," he said.

She held his gaze as her lips curled up into a smile.

"I didn't come here for softness, " she said.

His eyes blazed bright for a moment. Her jaw ached from the pressure of his touch, but she refused to show her discomfort. With a growl he released her chin and stood.

"Good to know we're on the same page," he said.

Touching his hand to his brow, he offered a mock salute.

His words were a direct contradiction to the heat smoldering in his gaze. She wondered if he knew his lies were so apparent. She'd witnessed him on the battlefield with death and rage plowing around him, while wielding his sword with absolute calmness and not a flicker of flame in his eyes. He prided himself on his control. Tonight she intended to strip him of every inch of it.

With a slight smile she raised an eyebrow and waited.

His heavy steps marched across the floor. The sound of clinking metal filled the air, making her muscles tense. When he returned, he held a pair of leather shackles held together by a short, thin chain. He dangled the restraints in front of her.

"You can walk away from this at any moment. One word from you and it will be over. Understand?"

She nodded.

"Your safe word is 'guilty'."

She raised her chin and pressed her lips into a firm line. His choice of safe word, delivered with a derisive smirk, was not lost on her.

"I won't need it," she said.

He squatted down and reached for her. Smoothing his hands down her arms, he circled her wrists.

"We'll see."

He pulled her wrists together in front of her and cinched the restraints closed around them. She curled her fingers down, surprised at how soft the material felt against her skin.

"Bend forward and spread your wings to your sides."

He tugged at the chain, and for the first time she noticed a small hook embedded on the floor before her. Swallowing against the dryness in her throat, she obeyed his command and leaned down, outstretching her arms.

He secured the chains around the hook and stood.

She trembled. The new position, forced her forehead and chest down to the floor, while exposing her ass and pussy. Her spread wings left her back bare to the air. It was a pose of supplication, and the knowledge of that sent liquid heat flooding to her core. She took a shuddering breath then bit back a groan as her sensitive nipples brushed the stone floor, the light abrasion stimulating the already hardened flesh.

Attempting to take shallow breaths, she focused on the sound of Dax moving around the room. She turned her head but couldn't see what he was doing. From the sounds of rustling and clinking filling the air, he was on the far side of the room again. Her heart beat sped up.

What is he doing?

"You said you wanted to atone—repent. We'll see how much guilt your conscious holds," he said.

His footsteps came closer and she sensed him pause behind her.

"Perfect," he whispered.

She jerked at the feel of a soft caress down her back.

"We'll start you off light," he said, "to see how much all this delicate skin can take."

The caress came again. It felt as if soft tendrils of velvet were stroking her skin. The coils moved down her spine and curved down her ass. Even though she knew it was a ploy, she couldn't prevent her body from relaxing into the soft touch.

He stroked her for several minutes. Each moment that passed created dual emotions within her. Fear of what would happen when the first strike hit her flesh, and arousal from the anticipation of feeling the first sting of the whip. Just as she began to melt into the stokes, a quiet swoosh of air was her only warning.

The first strike left her gasping. Pain exploded across her back. The soft tendrils that soothed her now created thin rivers of fire along her flesh. She tightened her hands around the chains and struggled to keep her breathing even. Pain radiated through her, followed by a slow pulse of pleasure. It swelled along the sting of her skin and settled into a throbbing ache at her core.

The whip snapped against her back again, this time trailing along her buttocks before lifting from her body. Her thighs clenched as arousal skittered along her nerves slicking her pussy with wet heat.

A new fear filled her now. How long would she be able to last before Dax discovered the truth?

Another bite of the whip landed, this time along the back of her thighs. Tears pricked her eyes, as she bit back a moan. Even as her conscious accepted the punishment her feelings of guilt demanded, her body craved the pleasure the pain provided.

Four

ax clenched his fists to avoid moving his hand down to his crotch and stroking his cock through his leathers.

Last night he'd welcomed the bargain Morgan proposed. It was their own wicked pact. An agreement that helped her assuage her guilt for killing Sigmund and his way proving she had no control over him. But standing there now he realized he'd made a desperate mistake.

His body tightened with each jerk of her body—each whimper she attempted to muffle.

Her skin shivered beneath the whip, dancing to a dark rhythm that enthralled him.

Gorgeous.

The beauty of it stole his breath. She knelt over in silence, her head bowed, and her hands wrapped tightly around the chains holding her bound.

He flicked the whip in his hand and watched her back curve. Satisfaction snaked through him at the sight. She didn't arch away from the lashes, she bowed into them.

"Do you need more Morgan?"

She remained silent and he smiled. Her panting filled the air and he crouched down to lift her chin, forcing her to meet his gaze.

Her cheeks were stained with tears, but her eyes were glazed over in lust. His cock hardened in response even as his lips curled in self-derision. Her pupils were dilated and her lips were puffy and slightly parted. She was the picture of arousal, and his whip had brought her to this state. Her response to pain was a delicious surprise.

"*Fuck*. You love this don't you?"

Her lips trembled and she shook her head in denial.

"No," she whispered.

"Your body is screaming differently," he said.

He hated that he reveled in that. Hated that his own body reacted to the way her own betrayed her. Dropping his gaze to her chest he licked his lips at the sight of her tightly pebbled nipples grazing the floor. The two pinpoints scraped the surface with each jerky breath she took. Raising his gaze back to hers, he smiled at the fear mingling with desire in her eyes.

Silent secrets.

That is how he would describe the emotions flickering across her face, and he wanted to uncover every dirty detail. Letting his powers loose again he elongated his other arm and transformed it into wisps of smoke. They laced around her body and circled around her heavy breasts before snaking down her stomach. When he reached the top of her mons he paused, stroking her there, letting the heat of his smoke pet her.

"Stop," she said.

Her voice trembled, and that aroused him further. Did she realize how much she gave away in the single panted word? He gripped her chin and smiled.

"Have you forgotten the rules already? We can stop right now. I'll unhook you and let you leave. But you won't be allowed back. Is that what you want?"

She bit her lip and shook her head.

"Good."

He continued with his exploration, his transformed arm caressing her skin, the heat of his smoke stroking her.

Her breathing hitched again, and the spark in her eyes intensified. Holding her gaze, he let the wisps travel further, wrapping around her upper thighs, and caging her pussy in heat. His tactile senses were heightened when he transformed, and the slippery wetness coating her inner thighs made his mouth water for a taste of her.

"*Ah.* There we are. All nice and wet aren't we?"

Her eyelids shivered for a moment, before she gave a reluctant nod.

"Answer me!"

He allowed the tufts to tighten around her, stroking and squeezing her breasts and thighs but the tendrils never touched her nipples or pussy. He denied them both that pleasure.

She responded with a groan.

" *Yes.*"

"Good. Do you want this to be part of our agreement Morgan? Do you need to be fucked until you can't remember what a vengeful bitch you are?"

His gut tightened at his harsh words, but he needed to distance himself from her and the need stretching his nerves tight.

She shook her head frantically, even as she arched into his touch. He let out a harsh laugh at her unspoken denial.

"We'll see."

He released her chin. Reaching over, he unhooked her shackles from the floor, then stood. Looking down, he admired her still body. Even amidst her denial, she maintained the position he'd ordered her in. He tugged at the chains.

"Stand," he said.

His smoke continued to slide around her, squeezing and caressing her as he guided her to the center of the chamber. She kept her gaze down to the floor the entire time. Dax wasn't sure whether she did so in order to be obedient, or if it was an attempt to hide her thoughts. Either way she would learn soon enough that while she was in this chamber, there was no hiding from him.

"Arms up."

She raised her hands above her head and he smiled at her quick acquiescence as he pulled the restraints over a large sturdy hook hanging from the ceiling. He admired her form for a moment. Her dusky breasts were turned upwards, and her longs legs framed her plump pussy.

Every fantasy he'd tried to work out of his system through shaping metal, roared through his mind and blazed straight to his cock. He wanted to turn those thighs red with his whip, then spread them wide and fuck her pussy raw.

He felt like a sick fuck. The exact type of fuck she said she needed help from.

"Look at me," he demanded.

She lifted her head in a reluctant swing.

"There are no lies here," he said. "If you don't tell me what you need. I can't give it to you. And if you lie about what you need, I *won't* give it to you."

She remained silent, offering him a stubborn glare.

So be it.

He uncoiled his smoke from her body, stroking her flesh as he retreated, unable to resist a quick swipe of her slit. She trembled at his ministrations, but didn't protest his withdrawal.

"I have the perfect toy for you. Something to get you in a truthful mood."

He walked over to a stone table and opened a slim ivory container. With a wicked smile, he removed an item from the box and returned to Morgan.

"Here we are," he said, waving the object in front of her face.

Her eyes opened wide, but still, she remained silent.

"Nothing to say? I admit it's not the largest tool in my arsenal, but it has some interesting benefits."

The object, a large dildo made of soft metal, was perfect for the game he planned on playing. Letting a small flame seep from his fingertips he heated the object until it warmed. The dildo was made from a combination of gold and glass, the formula allowed the material to stay warm for long periods of time. Dipping his hand, he placed the tip of the toy at her collarbone.

He traced it along her smooth skin, swirling it down to the top of her left breast before circling her nipple. He kept it there for a moment, enjoying the way her nipples tapped against the metal as her breathing became more uneven.

Imbuing the toy with more heat, he traced it down her stomach and stroked her mons with it.

She whimpered and arched her body, her back bowing and shifting her pussy closer to the toy.

Beautiful.

Unable to resist the bounty displayed beneath his nose, he dropped his head down to her chest and breathed in the heady scent caged between her breasts. He wrapped his arm around her waist and held her still, as he slid the toy down her labia and grazed her clit.

He loved the way she trembled against him, but refused to break. It was an aphrodisiac he couldn't resist.

"In we go," he whispered.

Turning his head, he snaked his tongue out and licked her nipple as he plunged the toy deep in her pussy.

She stilled for a moment, her body frozen in time, before she began to tremble and buck against him, her pussy gushing all over his fingers.

Her scream reverberated off the stone walls, prompting him to wrap his lips around her nipple and suck hard. She was delicious, her body coated with sweat and decadence.

He curled his hand over her pussy, teasing the rim of her entrance as his palm rubbed her clit. He didn't want her to come down from her release, he wanted to keep her right on the edge for as long as he could.

Her jerking movements subsided, but her hips continued to rock against his hand and little whimpers vibrated from her chest.

He looked up at her face, expecting to see shame or revulsion. Instead he saw only relief and hot desire.

We are a fucked up pair.

For a moment he felt a connection to her—a moment where he sympathized with her need to give up control. But he shoved the feeling aside.

"Now that we both know you were lying, it's time for your punishment," he said.

He withdrew the dildo and returned it to his bench. Clenching his jaw, he reminded himself, to not be swayed by his own desires. Feeling her shudder apart in his arms, to feel her wetness coat his hand, left him on shaky ground. Gritting his teeth, he walked to the far wall of the chamber and retrieved another whip. This one, a thin riding crop. Thinking of her thick thighs, he licked his lips. Striding back to her, he smiled.

"Unlike you, I have no intention of denying myself," he said.

He ran the tip of the crop along her inner thighs enjoying her shiver. With a quick flick of his wrist, he brought the crop down on her upper thigh. A bright slash of red mottled her skin, the bloom of color a gorgeous highlight. He'd been right, her thighs had been made for this.

He raised the crop again and smacked it against her other thigh. Now two perfect slashes marred her flesh bookending her beautiful pussy like a wicked set of parentheses. He struck her again and again, each strike making her flesh jump.

The way her skin bruised and mottled was mesmerizing.

"*Dax.*"

She said his name on a moan.

He looked up from his ministrations and his breath stilled. Her chest heaved and her back arched. Sweat dripped down her body and her inner thighs were slick and shiny.

She wasn't trembling in pain—she was on the brink of orgasm again. He lifted his wide gaze to hers. She licked her lips and whispered his downfall.

"Please."

His control snapped.

The crop fell from his hands as he dropped to his knees and wrapped her legs around his shoulders. Her pussy glistened with arousal, her clit peeking out between the two plump lips. Grabbing her ass, he stuck his tongue out and licked her slit. Her spicy flavor exploded across his tongue and he pulled her hips forward—shoving his face into the paradise between her legs. Wrapping his lips around her clit, he flicked it with his tongue before sucking on the succulent piece of flesh. She rewarded him with a loud scream and climaxing on his tongue.

He shoved his tongue into her pussy, wanting to savor every drop of her release. When her trembling began to ease, he licked and sucked at her flesh, his mouth watering for more of her taste. Swirling his tongue around her clit he glided a hand between her thighs and slid two fingers into her hot sheath.

Her inner muscles fluttered on his fingers and he curled them up, stroking the small group of nerves behind her clit. Setting a quick tempo, he tapped against the bundle as he stroked his tongue against her swollen nub. Her thighs clenched around his neck and fresh fluid coated his hand. He moaned against her flesh. It wasn't enough. He needed more.

Adding another finger to her pussy, he summoned his powers and allowed a small pulse of heat to warm his hand.

She froze against him, and another scream tore from her throat.

He moaned against her pussy, drunk on the arousal dripping from her core. His cock throbbed and swelled, his blood rushing to the engorged organ with each lick and suck. He curled his tongue into her, lapping up every drop her body released. He groaned against her, desperate for more. Her legs went lax around him, and low whimpering sounds filtered through his haze of desire.

Lifting his head, he stumbled to his feet and gaped down at her in shock even as he slicked his tongue out to lick his lips and savor the taste of her cum on his mouth.

"By the Gods," he whispered.

Wisps of her long dark hair clung to her sweat dampened skin. Her dark wings were spread wide behind her and her body still shivered with the aftermath of her release.

She was temptation personified.

Watching a bead of sweat trickle down her abdomen into the slick lips of her pussy, he wrestled with the last vestiges of his tattered control.

"Give me the word," he demanded, "make this end now."

She licked her lips and lifted her hunger filled gaze to his.

"Make me."

With a growl, he grabbed her hips, pulled her glistening body in his arms and claimed her lips in a searing kiss. She wrapped her legs around his waist—her slick pussy searing his stomach with her heat. He tore at his leathers and in one smooth movement, he thrust inside her.

I'm lost.

Moaning against her mouth, Dax admitted defeat. This small warrior had broken through every one of his defenses and now demanded tribute. Her legs tightened around him and he moved his hands down to her hips, holding her steady for his cock.

He pounded into her, invading her body and swallowing her breath all at once. He swore she stole a piece of his soul in those moments.

She groaned and writhed against him. Her pussy gushing hot and wet around his cock, squeezing confessions from his body that his mind fought to silence. Emotions he'd buried for months burst from him, pouring into her with each plunge through her tight cunt.

Lifting his head, he found her staring at him, her eyes reflecting the same need and devotion choking his heart.

With a guttural groan, he increased his tempo, his

thrusts becoming erratic. His power burst across his skin, engulfing them both in flickering flames. Her eyes widened and her pussy tightened around his flesh. She convulsed against him, her inner muscles clamping and milking at his cock. When her lips fell open on another scream, his cock swelled in an almost painful throb. He shouted as the first ropes of his release ripped from his body. He jerked against her, pushing balls deep, needing to fill her with every drop of his cum.

Watching her gasp for breath and tremble around him, only one thought reverberated through his mind.

Mine.

Five

Morgan struggled to catch her breath. Shivers raced down her skin as her body tried to recover from the firestorm that was Dax. Even with her rapid breaths, every cell in her body was relaxed with pleasure.

Her legs went limp around his waist, but Dax's iron grip held her to him, keeping their bodies joined.

She peered up at him, captivated by the low glow of flames hovering over his skin like a second skin. His eyes drooped low and his cheeks were flushed, giving him the look of a man thoroughly satisfied. She wanted to smile at the look, but apprehension began to invade her haze of contentment.

There was no way he didn't know the full truth now. She'd begged for his touch, reveled in it. Even if he didn't realize the depths of her feelings for him, he now knew she wanted him.

A part of her wanted to struggle against the chains and put enough distance between them so she could think clearly. Another part, was relieved that she wouldn't have to pretend anymore.

As if reading her mind, he smoothed a hand up her arms and wrapped his fingers around her wrists. The act pressed her chest against his. In defiance to her need to get away, her body reacted to the new contact. Her legs tightened around him and her pussy gave an interested flutter. She moaned and her eyes widened as she felt him harden inside her.

"You lied to me," he said.

Despite his clear arousal, his expression turned stoic. Releasing a soft breath, Morgan searched his eyes for any indication of his feelings.

"I told you the truth, just not the whole of it," she said.

"Now you're playing with semantics."

She shook her head.

"I didn't lie. I do feel guilty about Sigmund. I wish I had disobeyed my father and told you what was happening. You deserved to know."

With a sigh, he dipped his forehead down to press against hers.

"Sigmund deserved his fate. You did nothing wrong."

Confusion and hope warred within her.

"Do you really believe that?" she asked.

At his curt nod, her chest tightened.

"Then your refusal to speak to me..."

If he didn't blame her for Sigmund's death, why had he been pushing her away all these months?

"Vinghel, didn't trust me to take care of Sigmund myself because we were close. I can't afford to let emotions jeopardize my position again."

Emotions?

A surge of hope raced up her spine.

"What kind of emotions?" she asked.

His lips tightened.

"The kind that keep me unfocused and cause your father to not trust my skill," he said.

"No one ever doubted your ability to kill Sigmund. We both knew you would do what was necessary. Your code of honor would demand nothing less," she said.

"Then why didn't you tell me from the beginning?"

"Because we thought removing the choice would prevent you from feeling any remorse. We didn't hide the truth because we thought you weak. We did it because we knew you would carry out the task even if it hurt you."

The harsh lines of his face began to soften as he processed her words. She'd been a fool. All this time she struggled with getting him to forgive her, when he struggled to forgive himself for caring about a friend. She wished she'd come to him sooner and explained what happened. He didn't deserve to feel any shame.

"Do you think I'm weak?" she asked.

A look of surprise flickered across his face.

"You are one of the strongest warriors in the guard. It's an honor to fight beside you."

"But I have emotions," she said. "They give me the motivation to protect the people in my life—this world. I love my family, my friends...and a certain fire demon who's too stubborn to see me."

The moment the confession left her lips, relief spread through her. She relaxed against him. Releasing the words offered a relief from the constant pressure squeezing at her heart.

"*Love.*"

He hissed out the word, his face scrunching as if in pain. She wanted to smooth the deep lines, but offered him more truth instead.

"Yes, *love.* Every time I'm with you all I can think is how much I want you. How much I need your touch."

His cock pulsed inside of her, his flesh hardening and making her pussy clench around him. He muffled a curse and shook his head.

"Lust," he said, flexing his hips against her— grinding his hard shaft deeper inside her.

"No," she said, biting back a groan. She couldn't control her body's reaction. Her core heated and contracted around him, wanting more of the blaze of heat arcing through her core. "Lust would have me wanting you to fuck me. Love has me wanting to keep you buried inside me forever."

He moved his hands back down to her hips. His fingers dug into the flesh of her ass and twin flames sparked his eyes. Licking her lips, she continued.

"*Love* has me needing to uncover every piece of your soul that you keep hidden. To learn the things that make your hard face crack into a smile. To be an *emotion* you can't brush aside."

"Stop," he said between clenched teeth.

He thrust harder, burying himself to the hilt, stretching and filing her with rough strokes.

"I can't," she whispered. "I can't pretend, that I don't need you, that I don't crave everything you are. Every night I sleep, I dream about you being mine—about me being yours."

With a groan, he moved a hand to her neck and yanked on her hair, snapping her head back.

"You *are* mine," he said, his voice whipping out in a thick snarl.

A sharp second later his lips crushed hers.

She moaned into his mouth, loving the thick invasion of his tongue as his cock pounded into her. Wrenching his lips from hers, he licked a path down her neck, his teeth scraping against her collarbone before he nipped his way down to the center of her chest.

"You'll always be mine," he said against her skin, "If needing this—"

He turned his head and pressed a kiss to the inside of her left breast.

"If this is the consequence of my feelings, I can't let you go," he said.

Her heart burst at his declaration.

"Then don't," she said.

Pulling him close, she sighed at the feel of his hot skin beneath her hands. She curled her fingers along the back of his neck and tugged his head back, mimicking his earlier actions.

His lips curled up in a wicked smile as his cock throbbed inside her. He sank down to his knees and she settled around him, her thighs straddling his hips.

"You promised one night," he said, "and the night's not over."

"And when it is?" she asked.

He shook his head from her grasp. Dipping his head down to hers, he kissed the corner of her mouth. The delicate caress was a sexy contrast to the force of his thrusts.

"Then we can have one day—then another night," he said.

He nibbled across her lips to the other side.

"Then another day," he whispered.

Laughter bubbled up her throat and fell from her lips.

"That sounds like a long time," she said.

"Eternity usually works that way," he said.

Her laughter died on a moan as his mouth fused with hers again. Eternity sounded like a very good start.

The End

Turn the page for a sneak peek of the paranormal romance,
The Golden Pack Alphas *by Laurel Cremant.*

Chapter One

*P*rey always made the same mistake—they ran. Standing motionless at the floor-to-ceiling windows of his hotel room, Marcus Legrand looked out at the umbrella-dotted beach beyond. He savored the weight of anticipation and awareness that had cloaked him ever since he'd learned that Gigi had run—again.

A smile twitched his lips. She would never admit that, nor would she appreciate his use of the pet name he'd assigned to her. Strong-willed and stubborn, Georgia Walker never ran from anyone or anything—except him.

From the moment he'd first visited her pack, the prickly woman had loved to avoid and drive him crazy in equal measure.

As a High Council *Ma'at*, an enforcer of the laws and rites agreed upon hundreds of years ago by the original wolf packs, he preferred his life well-ordered. He knew all too well the chaos and destruction that came with flaunting pack rules.

He was that chaos. *He* was that destruction.

Gigi didn't seem to care. She was out there on the beach. No doubt celebrating her supposed coup in evading him.

It always amused him how easily a person underestimated a *were*—specifically a werewolf, and specifically *him*. But Gigi should have known better. As the daughter of Darius, the Golden Pack Alpha, she was more than privy to Council politics and the foolishness in taunting him. And yet, she did it anyway.

Her willingness to pick a fight stirred more than just the wolf in him—it woke the man. It had been a long time since any woman, shifter or otherwise, had aroused any interest in him. Even longer since one did more than make his cock twitch in interest. But from the moment he'd seen her and inhaled her heady scent, he'd wanted nothing else than to throw her over his shoulder and steal her away.

He'd been overwhelmed with that urge, and even now, after a year to come to terms with what it all meant, he struggled to tamp down on the compulsion to drag her to the nearest surface and fuck her until they both passed out into oblivion.

I have to catch her first.

Marcus gave a mental shrug. For him, the hunt was always the easy part. He reached up and ran his left hand along his opposite arm. Although covered by the thin layer of his shirt, he traced the fine lines of the tattoos beneath, every one as firmly etched into his memory as on his skin. Each symbolizing a kill or judgment made. Reminders of what he was, and the role he'd chosen to play.

Him being a lone wolf, the Council had recruited him years ago—more years than most knew. They'd taken him in, shielded his true origins, and in return, he'd become their hammer. The one they called upon to mete out justice. He'd never regretted his choice.

He understood the necessity of having a feared weapon on your side when approaching the bargaining table. Fear often created the best compromise. When the Council called upon his services, it signaled the end of negotiations.

He'd become accustomed to people watching him with unease and deference. Even the few women he engaged with were more interested in the thrill of sleeping with an enforcer than anything else. Yet, Georgia's eyes contained a different look entirely.

Her deep brown gaze challenged and aroused with each glance, each raise of the brow, and each drop of eyelashes.

Thinking back on the cool reception she'd given him when he'd first arrived in Golden Valley a year ago, the sadistic part of him smiled at his choice of conquest. Unlike other women, Gigi was not in awe of him. She didn't hold her tongue or pretend meekness. Her countenance screamed Alpha, and had his wolf—and another part of his anatomy—standing up to take notice from the start.

She'd stood at her father's side, tall and proud, her long dark hair falling around her shoulders in waves, framing toffee skin and high, rounded cheekbones. Her plush mouth had firmed in disdain and she'd quirked one delicate eyebrow at him.

"Oh, goodie. The new pit bull is here."

Her husky voice had delivered the cutting words without a single waver or pause. He'd noted it as possibly the sexiest thing he'd ever heard.

At first, he'd believed his reaction stemmed from her heat cycle. He could smell it on her—the thick musk of her arousal swirling through his senses, almost drowning him in the need to slant her stubborn chin up and sink his teeth into the succulent flesh of her neck.

Despite her obvious initial dislike of him, her eyes had flared with an answering blaze of attraction.

Meeting her had tilted his whole world off its axis, and things would never be the same for him.

Whether she deigned to admit it, they'd both chosen at that moment to withdraw to their respective corners. He'd come to the valley on official orders from the Council and had no time for small dalliances or otherwise. Whatever reasons she had for retreating remained her own.

He'd been sent to help deal with a rogue pack. Gigi's father, not wanting to endanger his own people, had called upon the Council to help settle the matter. Rogue wolves proved dangerous on several levels. Not only did they refuse to obey the rules set in place to protect *weres* from discovery, they also had no respect for life, human or otherwise.

Under normal circumstances, the Council would not have stepped in. Most rogue packs died a natural death. The absence of no true Alpha in the group always led to them killing each other off in a useless quest to dominate.

But this pack had been different. On top of deliberately breaking the rules, they'd begun kidnapping humans and turning them. That, the Council could not ignore.

Dealing with them hadn't taken much time. But there had been some casualties, one of them being Darius' Beta. In the end, the group had been defeated and dispatched, justice met, and his job done—seven new feathers added to his collection. However, during his stay, he'd developed an attachment to the Golden Pack that had been...unexpected.

After delivering his report to the Council, Marcus had returned to Golden Valley—and to Gigi.

As an enforcer, he had the right to set up base wherever he chose, and for the time being, he'd settled on the biting cold mountains of Golden Valley. He'd even agreed to play temporary Beta to Darius.

He liked the pushy Alpha. His twinkling eyes, booming voice, and ready smile could too easily be misconstrued as trusting and easy-going, but Marcus had seen him in battle. Darius proved to be one of the shrewdest wolves he'd ever encountered—and deadliest. Traits he had no doubt passed down to his only daughter.

The dynamic between Darius and the other wolves intrigued him.

None in the group resented their Alpha's choice in mate, Genevieve, Gigi's mother. Her being a witch didn't seem to bother the other wolves. Yet, for some, he'd seen that an obvious weariness of Gigi herself existed.

Her hybrid status put them on edge. A part of them questioned her right to belong. In that, he could sympathize with her. He understood the difficulties of being different in a world that expected sameness.

It felt strange to him—being surrounded by a collective. The feeling wasn't entirely bad. Just different.

He'd never given any consideration to becoming part of any one pack. Both his history and need for privacy didn't lend themselves to community living.

Yet, he'd stayed. He'd set up house in a small bungalow close to Darius' large home. He'd chosen the location in small part to be available to Darius and in larger part to be near Gigi—her cottage being only a few yards on the other side of the main house. Each day, he grew more attached to the land, and each day, he wanted Gigi with a need that bordered on obsession.

She avoided him, evaded his presence with a skill he had to admire. He reveled in their power struggle.

Just before her recent disappearing act, he'd found her leaving her father's office, back straight and eyes flashing.

"Bad day?"

"Fuck off."

"Such a lady."

"And you're such a pest."

He reached out and touched her arm, pausing her marching progression.

"In a suicidal mood today?" she asked.

"With you? Always. Now tell me what has you so upset."

Her nostrils flared and she leaned into him.

"You. You bother me. When are you going to saddle up and find yourself a new pack to annoy?"

"Maybe as soon as you stop running."

Her lips curled up in a sneer.

"I don't run from anyone, Legrand. If I choose to not be around you, it means that I see no need in spending time with arrogant pricks."

He stroked a hand up her waist and brushed a fingertip over one tight nipple.

"And yet, those sensitive nipples of yours say differently every time I see you."

She returned the favor, running a hand down his front and cupped his hard cock.

"And your dick seems to have the same problem," she said, her voice almost sickly sweet.

Their gazes held as he pinched her nipple, and she squeezed his shaft.

"It would be a shame for you if I had to rip it off," she whispered before wrenching away from his hold and storming away.

He'd watched her walk away with a smile on his face. Even the threat of dismemberment hadn't been enough for his arousal to subside. He considered each encounter with her as progress. Soon, she would admit that there was more between them than just simple attraction.

Focusing back on the beach, he narrowed his gaze onto a specific pink umbrella poised haphazardly in the sand.

He touched a hand to his suit pocket, feeling the note folded inside. Darius had requested that he bring Gigi home for Christmas. But even if Darius hadn't asked him to find Gigi, Marcus would have come for her. They'd spent the last year tiptoeing around each other, and it had to stop.

Dropping his hands down to his sides, he turned from the window and strode to the door. Time to go hunting.

Chapter two

Sunshine, rum punch, and hot men.

Hell, yeah.

Georgia Walker smiled—a contented sigh drifting across her lips as she adjusted the thin straps of her red and white bikini top. Nothing could compare to celebrating Christmas in the Caribbean.

No concerns over urgent emails, emergency meetings, or irate clients—and most importantly, she didn't have to worry about the pressure of being a pack Alpha's daughter or combat the suspicious looks of those who didn't trust her hybrid birth.

Being born to both a witch and a *were* came with certain privileges and drawbacks.

On one hand, she had the strength and stamina of a wolf; on the other, her ability to sense when others lied made more than one pack member wary. The fact that the usual dose of instinct and intuition shifters were normally gifted with became intensified by her mother's shaman heritage only seemed to make matters worse.

Not to mention her parents' recent penchant for matchmaking. She shuddered at the thought of being paraded around a room full of want-to-be Alphas. Lately, she could practically see thought bubbles of grandchildren floating around her mom's head.

So given a choice, she much preferred her current location rather than the week of holiday social events her mother planned every year with military precision.

About a two hours' drive east of Vancouver, her hometown, Golden Valley, sat nestled between tall, rolling mountains and crisp, dense green forests. She would always consider it home, but she had to admit that her current view on the beach held more than a little appeal.

Reclining back on her lounge chair, she closed her eyes and let the warmth of the sun sink into her bones.

The limb-freezing climate of British Columbia in winter had nothing on the powder-soft sandy beaches, warm, clear-blue waters, and cool breezes of Jost Van Dyke.

She'd discovered the little island paradise a year ago while on a case and had never been so happy to stake out a cheating husband.

Her business, a private security and detective firm,

had grown a lot in the last five years, and she rarely went on cases herself anymore, but she'd made an exception for her best friend, Kara. Georgia didn't make friends easily—a byproduct of spending most of her days either focused on building up her company or on pack politics. But when she'd hired Kara several years ago as an Internet security specialist, the quirky human had wormed her way into Georgia's heart.

When Kara had confided to her that she suspected her husband of cheating, Georgia had handled the investigation personally.

Although she'd returned home to deliver divorce-inducing news, she had done so with sun-streaked hair and a deeper tint to her brown skin.

Now, thanks to a few new lucrative contracts, she'd had no qualms in splurging on a last-minute vacation.

She looked forward to a few days without worrying about urgent emails, pack politics, and being away from *him*.

Marcus Legrand.

From the moment he'd stepped foot in Golden Valley, the tight-backed enforcer had set off clanging alarm bells to the tune of Iron Maiden's *The Number of the Beast* in her mind.

She reacted to him in a way she was woman enough to admit scared her almost witless.

Her usual abilities of intuition rang silent when it came to him. As if he'd constructed a lead wall around his mind and she couldn't get a read on him—ever.

She couldn't even anticipate his approaches, and he seemed to revel in his ability to sneak up on her.

But when he was near—her body went on high alert, as if it had been starved for him, and she didn't like it one bit.

When he'd first arrived a year ago, she'd been about to start her heat cycle and meeting him had hurtled her body head first into estrous.

Marcus embodied everything she'd fought against her entire life—loss of control.

From a young age, she'd always strived for discipline over the urges her wolf and animal nature pushed on her. It was no secret that she was quick to temper, but few ever provoked her to the point of violence. Thanks to her quick wit and gift of clairvoyance, the use of intimidation and fear became her weapons of choice.

Her choice in path had more to do with self-preservation than any lofty ideas on violence.

She'd known early on that her wolf was strong, stronger than even her parents suspected. But a faction of wolves within the community were already suspicious of her. If they learned how much power she truly had, she would never be able to win them over.

The pack was all the family she had. Her mother had been an only child, and the coven she'd once belonged to had shunned her when she chose to mate with Georgia's father.

But all that didn't matter. Given a choice, she would always choose her pack.

Georgia had grown up in pack life and her wolf craved a sense of community. She would do anything to maintain that connection.

For that reason, she rarely shifted and would seldom be found during the group runs and hunts the pack engaged in. Remaining in her human form allowed her to avoid detection. Contrary to human myths and legends, werewolves weren't compelled to shift during full moon phases. The ability could be controlled except for the rare exceptions of *weres* with mental illnesses and instabilities.

She recalled the last time she'd shifted—during the rogue attacks the year before. Not only had it been the first time she'd shifted in months, it had also been the first time she'd seen Marcus' wolf.

Her father had assembled a small group of fighters, their goal not to engage the rogues but only to surround their camp while Marcus investigated. They'd gathered just outside of the forest surrounding Golden Valley, eager to route the unwanted wolves from their home territory.

Turning her back, she'd allowed her body contort slowly, making sure not to let her power flare. The others had shifted around her and she'd expected to feel the excitement that always occurred when her wolf recognized the chance to be free—at least for a moment. But this time, a burst of elation had burst through her heart so strong it had left her frozen in shock.

Her wolf had blazed a myriad of thoughts and images through her mind, but only one word had come through crystal clear.

Mate.

She'd leapt around, her gaze drawn to only one wolf—Marcus.

Her heart thrummed fast as she recalled the image of his wolf. He'd been beautiful. In that moment, she'd seen why the Council had chosen him as enforcer.

Large and hulking, his wolf almost resembled a bear. Even his fur was intimidating, spiked brown with blond tips, reminding her of sharpened spikes.

Shaking her head clear, she came back to the present.

Marcus was lethal in more than just his skills as an enforcer.

She refused to let her destiny be determined by a chemical impulse to mate, and his presence threatened the hard-won control she'd spent years honing.

The unfairness of it all galled her. The decision of who she spent the rest of her life with should be made by *her*. Not her overzealous wolf, and definitely not some hormonal urge.

Each day, her irritation grew as it became more difficult not to succumb to the urge of crawling onto the man's lap and sating the unending hunger that had been building since they'd first met.

All of that didn't matter now. For the next several days, she would be free from the worries that plagued her at home.

Taking a deep breath, she reached her arms overhead, arched her back, and inhaled the balmy salted air.

She could almost hear her muscles sigh, but despite the relaxation attempting to spread through her limbs, her body tingled with a tension settled too deep.

Her heat cycle was starting—nothing she could do to relieve the discomfort.

Well, almost nothing.

Dropping her hands back down to her sides, she swept her gaze across the small beach. It wasn't crowded but had a fair number of sunbathers and Zen cravers. And most importantly, it had men looking for the same thing she was—a little fun, forgetfulness, and zero strings.

Although heat pooled to her center, her stomach rolled in apprehension.

In the past, she'd had no problems finding a willing male to sleep with when she was in heat. She enjoyed sex, and although each year, her parents hoped she would choose a permanent mate, no man in or outside of her pack inspired much feeling or devotion. At least, not enough for her to be shackled to for life.

But since last year, because of *The-Wolf-Who-Shall-Not-Be-Named*, no one appealed to her.

Instead of rolling around for several hours with a well-endowed chosen playmate, she'd remained locked in her home for days with her vibrator and a healthy supply of batteries.

She had no intentions of repeating the experience. This week, she planned on proving to both her body and wolf that Marcus wasn't the only man capable of making her hot.

Her gaze combed the area, looking for a good candidate.

One particular man caught her eye.

He'd been swimming for the last hour, his caramel arms cutting through the water in languid strokes. But now, he rose out of the surf resembling a naughty sea nymph, his strong legs leading up to deep blue board shorts. Dry, she guessed the swimming trunks were perfectly modest—but wet, they molded to his thick, muscled thighs and cupped his cock in a way that left very little to the imagination. And since Georgia's imagination was better than the average wolf's, she bit back a groan and clenched her thighs tight.

Yum.

Pushing her sunglasses up to her hair, she licked her

lips as her gaze traced the diamond-bright droplets of water running along his hard chest. They sluiced down his body, aided by the tight ridges of muscles along his abdomen, tunneling down to what looked like one hell of a stocking stuffer.

Merry Christmas to me.

Yes, an island getaway was proving to be the perfect holiday treat.

Her gaze meandered back up his chest and after taking a brief note of thick smooth lips and tempting dimples, she made eye contact with her merman come to life.

His eyes gleamed with interest and her lips turned up in her best come-hither smile. He took a step forward and then froze, his gaze focusing on something just over her left shoulder. Shaking his head, he turned and continued walking down the beach.

What the hell!

She frowned at his retreating back. Admittedly, she was no supermodel, but she'd never had a problem with luring men her way.

A long shadow fell over her.

Her turn to freeze. Despite him blocking out the sun, a heated scorch rippled down her torso and limbs as the approaching shade crept down her body. Her nipples pebbled to thick points, her pussy clenched, and a slow growl worked its way up her throat.

Only one thing made her body react this way, and she'd deliberately left it back in Golden Valley.

"Hello, Gigi. Miss me?"

* * *

THE GOLDEN PACK ALPHAS
Available now via all major book retailers.

Turn the page for a sneak peek of the contemporary romance, RAPT *by Laurel Cremant.*

Chapter One

"Will you walk into my parlour?" said the Spider to the fly.

Lucas Wright smiled as he thought of the line from an old children's fable. He'd never considered himself a predator, but the ever-pressing need to devour one Ms. Jessica Wright convinced him otherwise. For almost a year, he had wanted nothing more than to drag her to his bed and wrap her in so much pleasure she'd never leave.

He shook his head derisively as he stood up from his workout mat. Sweat dripped down his bare chest and abdomen. Even after almost two exhausting hours of intense yoga, his muscles tightened and his cock stirred to attention at the image of her forming in his mind, all bothered and wet, stretched out on his bed.

Soon.

Today, he planned to take action.

He walked to edge of his hotel suite and stepped out onto the large glass rimmed balcony. Pulling in a deep breath, he let the warm salty breeze of the Fort Lauderdale coastline fill his lungs and calm his building anticipation. By tonight, he would know for sure whether Jessica was willing to take their flirtations to another level.

If she's honest with herself.

And that was the crux of it. He wondered if she was ready to admit that they'd both been playing a long drawn out game for quite some time. Each of them pushing the boundaries of their professional relationship and testing the waters. For months, they had danced around each other, whether Jessica chose to admit it or not. In the beginning, he'd almost missed it. Caught up in his own need to control his attraction and baser instincts he'd almost missed the signs.

Lucas hired her to be his chief acquisitions actuary. His company specialized in mergers and acquisitions. When his previous actuary retired, Jessica had come highly recommended. Upon reviewing her resume, he noted she was bright, driven, and after interviewing her for over an hour, he'd added tenacious and perfect for the job to her list of qualifications.

However, from the moment Jessica stepped into his office he'd wanted her for more than just her skills in the field. She'd reminded him of a painting he purchased several years before. Titled Calypso, the picture depicted a curvaceous, naked black woman sprawled on a throne, her head turned as she stared out at the ocean. One leg dangled over the side of the chair while the other trailed on the floor, her feet pointed and delicate looking. The painting had hit him like a punch to the gut and he'd purchased it on the spot. The first time he met Jessica he had the same reaction.

He'd been instantly attracted by the soft lush curves hugged underneath her deep gray pencil skirt. The full pout of her full lips as she spoke to him in a soft husky voice had him aroused in seconds and the creamy smoothness of her chocolate skin had him itching to reach out and test its softness. Every inch of her seemed designed to entice him— from her warm brown eyes, down her luscious body, to the point of her stiletto-heeled shoes. She exuded a combination of confidence and intelligence that only added to her allure. However, at the age of thirty-eight, he'd learned enough in his lifetime to not to let attraction get in the way of business.

He had a hard and staunch rule of never mixing business with pleasure. Aside from it just being a sound business practice, his rule allowed him to maintain a certain level of privacy. One of the pitfalls of owning a company as large as his was that people became inordinately interested in his personal life. Since he had no intention of handing over his business or going broke anytime soon—it was drawback to success he accepted whole-heartedly.

His sexual preferences were also a part of his need for privacy. Although he didn't fully immerse himself into the world of BDSM, he'd learned a long time ago that he was a moderate sexual sadist. Unlike most people, his revelation didn't come as an epiphany or gradual understanding of his psyche. Growing up with two college professors as parents he was surrounded by scientific and medical journals his entire life. By the time he had his first sexual experience, he'd recognized and accepted his sexuality. He'd even had a few rather frank discussions with his parents regarding the matter. Being the child of two very progressive, former hippie parents had its advantages.

However, embracing his sexuality didn't mean he wanted it open to public discussion. He was very selective in choosing lovers. Although he didn't find it difficult to find women willing to dabble in his lifestyle, over the last few years he wanted more and more a woman willing to play long-term.

The clock is ticking.

He smiled derisively at that thought. Lately he'd felt as if time was ticking by too quickly. He'd grown up an only child and had always wanted a large family. Although he wanted a woman willing to submit her pleasure to him in bed, he also wanted a strong female role model for his future children. He looked back on the long drawn out discussions his parents would have at the dinner table with fondness. They discussed everything from movies to global geopolitics with passion and he wanted that same type of relationship with the woman he chose to marry. Finding that woman seemed easier said than done—until he'd met Jessica.

Jessica had surprised him. Not only did he find the tall, dark beauty sexy, he appreciated her keen intelligence and sharp wit. Every now and then he would sense vulnerability in her, but her take charge, no-nonsense personality masked any softness well. That combination of hard and soft intrigued him and had the sadist and him, among other things, standing at attention.

She personified the type of woman he wanted to pursue and so much more. It took him a while to admit that he'd fallen for her but something about her tugged at him, making it difficult for him to ignore. His stance of not mixing business with pleasure had been the only thing holding him back. However, all that changed when he realized, Jessica was fighting the same attraction. Not only that—she also seemed to enjoy the mounting sexual tension as much as he did. It seemed his sexy actuary exhibited a touch of sexual masochism.

It started small. He'd notice her long glances down his body when she thought no one was looking, her hitched breathing as their meetings progressed—the hard pebbling of her nipples beneath her blouse. He'd recognized those signs.

When he first began exploring the BDSM lifestyle, he'd encountered more than a few masochists who enjoyed prolonging sexual stimulation. One woman in particular enjoyed masturbating for days prior to seeking any relief. He could see her glassy eyed arousal mirrored in Jessica's behavior as the months progressed.

He began anticipating each meeting with her. Testing her limits by prolonging their discussions and watching her body tighten and squirm with each passing minute. The air hung heavy with the scent of her arousal—the ultimate aphrodisiac. He'd inhaled the scent his mouth watering at the implication. He marveled that she thought he wouldn't notice how aroused she was as she sat in front of him, crossing and uncrossing her legs every few minutes. He dragged that meeting out—the sadist in him couldn't help it—and watched as her breath caught repeatedly.

When he finally decided to end the meeting, she stood on shaky legs as he escorted her out of the office. Even after tormenting her for so long he couldn't resist the urge to confirm his suspicions. As he'd reached to open the door, he deliberately grazed his arm against the front of her blouse, sweeping across her hard nipples. Her slick lips fell open on a gasp, and her eyes had blazed with an almost crazed passion.

He let her escape that day with a murmured apology, he'd watched her stumble down the hall to her office and slam the door shut—his lips curling up in a wide grin.

There was nothing a sadist liked better than a game of denial and patience.

He'd been playing the same game ever since. Knowing she was aroused, prolonging meetings to see just how long she could last. Their meetings were becoming an addiction for him and fantasizing about what she did each time she left him kept his body on overdrive and caused more than a few sleepless nights.

Not many women were into his preferred method of sexual dominance. His brand of sadism focused almost exclusively on sexual denial—on having a woman submit control to him and allowing him to decide when they would receive pleasure. The slow delay or denial of pleasure and gradual buildup of arousal gave him the power to deconstruct a person's orgasm. That type of power dynamic and play turned him on like nothing else. Finding a partner to indulge with proved more difficult than most people would think.

Most women loved the concept of extended foreplay, but when he prolonged it passed an hour or more without allowing them to come, they weren't exactly happy to meet his acquaintance.

Leaning his elbows on the railing, he stared out over the small crowd of sunbathers and tourists below on the beach, his gaze resting the perfect cerulean blue of the ocean beyond.

Lucas recalled the brief emails she'd exchanged with him that day and released a short breath. Her current assignment was over and as usual, she would make her way to him to deliver her final report and analysis in person. In a little over an hour Jessica would arrive and the anticipation of it was already tightening his skin and heating his blood. To tell the truth he'd been running on high since the moment she'd messaged him earlier in the day. He'd prolonged his yoga routine in the hopes of exhausting his body and diminishing his libido.

No such luck.

He should have known better. Pushing back from the rail, he turned and walked back into his suite and stretched his arms over head, trying to release the mounting tension spreading across his shoulders. Dropping his hands down to his waist he untied his drawstring pants and let them fall to the floor before making his way into the bathroom. He stepped into the cool marble shower enclosure and locked his knees tight before twisting on the water.

He whispered a soft curse as cold water sluiced down his body. As the freezing water beat down on his skin, Lucas consoled himself with a single thought. Tonight he would either find relief or learn definitively that Jessica was hands off.

* * *

The office smelled like sex—again.

Jessica Wright cut her gaze to the flustered woman holding the door open for her. The woman's lips were swollen and bare of lipstick while her high cheekbones were tinged a bright hue of red. All of that, combined with the woman's mussed hair and rumpled clothing, left Jessica with no doubt that the woman and the man sitting smugly at his desk had just engaged in some extracurricular office activity.

I don't get paid enough for this.

Releasing her breath in a quick huff, Jessica stepped over the threshold into the sleek office of Shepard Electronics CEO, Richard Planks. The door closed with a soft snick behind her. Despite her disgust for Planks, she couldn't keep her pulse from speeding up in anticipation. Not for her meeting with Planks but for what would happen afterward. Dealing with Planks now meant she would see Lucas Wright later.

Lucas Wright. Her current employer and guilty pleasure. Because of him her usual enjoyment of dealing with scum like Planks was heightened with the knowledge that seeing Wright always followed. Tingling pinpricks raced across her skin and her palms began to sweat. Suppressing the need to rub them down the sides of her skirt she kept her gaze trained on Planks.

"I hope I didn't interrupt anything important," she said as she walked towards him.

"Nothing that couldn't be rescheduled," he replied in the

low nasal drawl indicative of his Bostonian roots.

Oh, I'm sure.

He didn't rise from his seat as she entered the room. Not that she expected him to. The man was sleazy arrogance personified. He'd made it clear since she first arrived several weeks ago, that he wasn't worried about what her investigation might find. That didn't surprise her. In her line of work, she'd found that regardless of level of wealth—greed and hubris were equal opportunity vices amongst people in powerful positions.

Richard Planks indulged in both to the point of addiction.

He sat at his desk, his tailored suite rumpled, a satisfied smile twitching at his lips. She wondered for the hundredth time, how a man so stupid managed to become CEO of such a large corporation. She'd perused thousands of financial data proving her assessment. Richard Planks wasn't only a sleaze—he was also a thief and a cheat. And the man truly believed his machinations wouldn't be discovered.

Fool.

She didn't wait for permission to be seated. Planks wasn't the type to extend an invitation. He liked people to feel uncomfortable around him. Jessica had no patience for his silly power play. Sitting down, she leaned back into the soft leather chair and crossed her legs. She watched as his gaze followed the movement of her legs, lingering for a moment on the small stretch of thigh revealed by the hem of her skirt. The leer curling across his features didn't bother her. It only served to make the moment to come so much sweeter.

Her lips trembled as she tried to keep a wide smile from stretching across her mouth. This was the part of her job she loved the most—the moment when smug men like Planks were gob-smacked with truth.

She'd spent years studying and training to become an actuary and for the last year she'd had the exclusive pleasure of being Lucas Wright's acquisitions actuary. Her main job function was to investigate the viability of companies like Shepard Electronics and determine whether they were worth Wright's time and money to acquire. Most people assumed that the world of mergers and acquisitions was all about hostile takeovers, but a good portion of the deals were mutual and in Planks case much welcomed.

Obviously, he couldn't wait to shake himself of his burgeoning electronic firm. His eagerness wouldn't normally be a red flag. Some people were honest enough with themselves to know when they'd taken their companies as far as their abilities and assets allowed. Yet from their first meeting Jessica knew Planks was far from humble. No—his eagerness to be acquired by Wright Inc. had little to do with humility and everything to do with greed and like most men of his ilk, he assumed that no one would figure out his schemes.

"I hope you've found everything you need."

He said the words in dismissive nonchalance fueling her excitement.

She smoothed her thumb along the file folder in her hand. It contained a copy of her final report, detailing the viability of Planks' company and whether or not it represented a good investment.

This is going to be fun.

"Yes. Actually, I was able to complete my final analysis this afternoon. I sent it over to Mr. Wright before coming to see you," she said.

"Wonderful. I'll let my lawyers know to begin the paperwork so that we can move forward."

"That won't be necessary." She leaned forward and placed the file on the desk.

"Mr. Wright has elected to withdraw his bid for Shepard Electronics."

She watched as her words penetrated the thick fog of arrogance surrounding him. It didn't take long. His eyes widened for a brief moment before narrowing in anger while his smirking lips firmed into a grim line.

"What the hell are you talking about?"

He jacked forward in his chair and snatched the file open. His gaze blazing across the lines she'd enjoyed typing with relish.

Satisfaction skittered through her. Yes—moments like these were exactly why she loved her job. Some children grew up wanting to be doctors, firefighters or astronauts. She'd grown up wanting to make men like Planks wallow in their own failure.

A therapist might say her satisfaction stemmed from a childhood filled with disappointments caused by inattentive socialite parents, along with a dose of resentment at being abandoned. After authorities discovered their lavish lifestyle had been funded by a myriad of embezzlement and Ponzi schemes her parents fled the country in fear of imprisonment. Had they repented in any way? No. They merely chose a country with no extradition agreements with the United States and continued to live without care for their actions or daughter. Since Jessica was well aware of her motivations and baggage, she had no problem with forgoing potentially massive therapy bills for the lucrative six-figure salary she received by taking men like Planks down instead.

"I found the transfers. It took me a little while, but the thing about money is that it always leaves a trail. No business is squeaky clean, but those hefty deposits you've been moving into your accounts..."

She shook her head and pursed her lips—letting out a short tsking sound.

"Not a very smart move. So I'm sure you can understand why Mr. Wright wouldn't want to move forward with a company whose profit margins have been faked for the last six quarters," she said.

The crunching sound of paper rent the air as his fist

clenched around the file. His knuckles paled into a glowing white; a stark contrast to the deep red flush racing up his neck to cover his scowling face in an angry mask.

"You fucking bitch!"

She raised an eyebrow at his snarled accusation.

Typical.

It never ceased to amaze her how easy some people found it necessary to resort to name-calling. On some level, she appreciated the last attempt at a jab. After all, in Planks' case she had just guaranteed that his family and colleagues would learn of his dirty dealings.

"Thank you," she said as she rose from her seat.

He leapt to his feet and leaned forward—bracing his hands down on the desk.

"You can't do this!"

Her gaze flicked down his body briefly before meeting his eyes dead on.

"I just did."

She turned on her heel and walked to the door—a string of expletives and curses raining down her back as she reached for the knob. She paused for a moment there.

"By the way. You might want to wipe the lipstick stains from your slacks before you go meet with your board of directors."

With that, she strode from the office, her only thoughts focused on seeing Lucas again.

* * *

RAPT

Available now via all major book retailers.

Laurel Cremant

Laurel is a romance author, who like most writers loves to read. Her first love (pun intended) has always been romance. From the sappy YA romance novel to the more risqué erotica novels, Laurel is a sucker for a good love story.

After spending years working in science and data, in 2011 Laurel decided to finally put her love of romance and the written word to good use. With a love for   romantic tension and snarky heroines, she penned her first romance novel and hasn't looked back.

Laurel writes paranormal and contemporary romance and is a self-proclaimed, out of the closet nerd. She admits that she can't seem to avoid adding a bit of "nerdology" or "geek-dom" to all of her books. Living in Miami, she also admits that she can't seem to avoid giving her heroines gorgeous shoes, "In Miami, we worship everything strappy, open toed and just plain hot!"

www.LaurelCremant.com

Other Books by Laurel Cremant

<u>Contemporary</u>
Mistletoe Dreams

Persuasion Skills

Negotiating Skills

Rapt

<u>Paranormal & Urban Fantasy</u>
Death's Hope (Dark Submissions I)

Guilt's Pleasure (Dark Submissions II)